# Deputy Sean

## Haven Island PD: Protecting Paradise

Neri Lopez

Siren Book & Craft LLC

Copyright © 2025 by Neri Lopez
Publisher: Siren Book & Craft LLC
Editor: Michelle Zammataro
Cover designer: Neri Lopez
Cover image: Neri's Beach Photo, Vecteezy, and Depositphotos
Maps are fictional and designed by Neri Lopez with images from Vecteezy

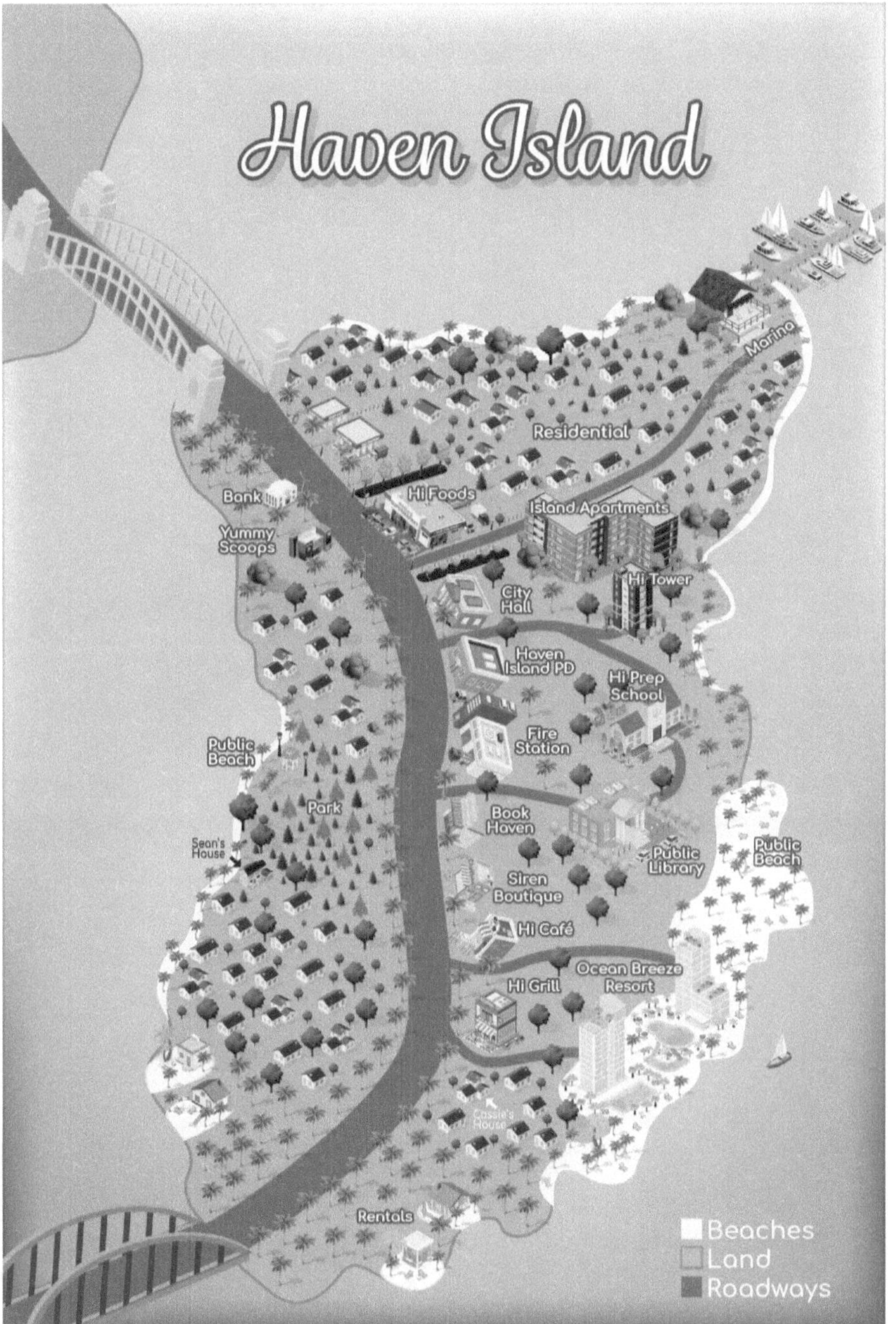

Haven Island
Marina
Residential
Bank
Hi Foods
Island Apartments
Yummy Scoops
Hi Tower
City Hall
Haven Island PD
Hi Prep School
Fire Station
Public Beach
Park
Book Haven
Sean's House
Public Library
Public Beach
Siren Boutique
Hi Café
Ocean Breeze Resort
Hi Grill
Cassie's House
Rentals
Beaches
Land
Roadways

# Contents

## Chapter 1

# I Hate Goodbyes

## Sean

"**C**hug, chug, chug, chug!"

The crowd chanted as I finished what I hoped would be my last beer of the night. George, my partner and best friend in South Florida, not only convinced me to have drinks on my last night in South Florida, but he also persuaded the entire group to join us. I wasn't as close to them as George, but I always enjoyed spending time with them. Even when I had to break up bar fights, because the girls demanded their infamous nights out. Their first rule was no boyfriends or husbands allowed.

Naturally, that rule didn't last after the first bar fight. Then Mark became their chaperone, because all the other men would bail on him, just to fuck with him. Mark would attempt to keep the peace, but eventually the police would be called, and George and I would show up for backup.

Thunder, Grayhorse, Mark, Alex, Barrett, and Holt were the guys in our group. Their significant others, in respective order, were Isa, Sarah, Maggie, Tori, Angel, and Freya. Although George introduced Thunder as his brother, I learned later that they were not blood relatives. Thunder was his mentor when he was in a boy's shelter. Grayhorse, was married to Thunder's sister Sarah and was Thunder's brother-in-law. Mark, Maggie, Alex, and Tori all worked with Thunder at the American Indian Cultural Center. Mark and Maggie were engaged; Tori and Alex were married. Barrett was married to Angel and Holt to Freya. Barrett, Holt, and Freya were casino employees. Since the Rock 'n' Roll Resort & Casino was part of my beat, I was very familiar with it.

It was supposed to be a guys' night out, but the women insisted on joining the going-away party. Since Maggie was using crutches, Mark jumped at the chance to have the party at his house rather than a bar. Every one of his friends' girlfriends, fiancées, or wives was breathtakingly beautiful, with their elegant dresses and sparkling jewelry, and he always grumbled about being their designated protector.

Hearing Mark volunteer his house was like a weight lifting from my shoulders—I really didn't want to risk running into Kerri and her new boyfriend at the bar with my friends. Kerri and I had dated for two fucking years. She even begged me to take a desk job because she hated the thought of someone knocking on our door telling her I'd died in the line of duty.

We'd been arguing constantly, the tension thick in the air, and I hoped a nice lunch would ease things, but when I got home, I found them. Kerri was being screwed doggy style on our bed by one of the many gym rats. Not being able to believe what I was seeing, I stood there frozen, watching him plowing into her while she moaned loudly, letting him know how much she enjoyed it. Fuck, I couldn't look away from the shock of what I was seeing. My heart felt like it was being ripped in two, a searing, furious energy coursing through me, threatening to consume them in a fiery blaze. My fists clenched tight, knuckles white, the pressure building until my fingers throbbed with pain. Neither one of them noticed me until I heard them climax and the asshole landed on top of her.

*"Oh my God, Sean," Kerri said when she finally opened her eyes and turned her head in my direction. She then pushed the guy off her and attempted to wrap herself up in the* bedsheet.

*"Hey, man," the asshole gym rat scurried to the side of the* bed, *far away from me. "It's not what you think."*

*"You mean you weren't just fucking my girlfriend in our fucking bed?" My eye twitched from all the anger I had inside.*

*"Sean." Kerri stood in front of him and placed a hand on his chest. "Thad means nothing to me."*

*"From the sounds of your voice and the thrusting of your body, it seems to me he means something. Because why else would I walk into our bedroom hoping to take my girlfriend to lunch and find the two of you grinding into each other?" I was surprised by how calm my voice sounded when all I wanted to do was rip Thad's head off. Thad must've seen the fury etched onto my face, because he scrambled for his clothes and fled into the bathroom.*

*"Well, you're never home, and I got lonely." Kerri spat out while she crossed her arms, holding the sheet.*

*"Lonely, my ass. I come home every night, and I spend all my days off with you. Get your shit and go. I never want to see you again."*

*"Sean, let's talk." Kerri pleaded. But I wasn't in the mood for her lies. I held up my hand to shut her up and glared at her. "Get your shit and go. I don't want to see you when I get home from my shift."*

With that said, I ignored all her ranting and raving while I stormed out of the house. After my shift, I dreaded going home. Luckily, when I went inside and walked around my house, she had moved everything out, including some of my things. Her betrayal had cut deep. Seeing her every day had been the highlight of my days and nights. The house now felt so empty and quiet.

For the next few months, I stared at the empty rooms and walls, wondering what the fuck I'd done wrong. I gave Kerri everything I had to give. Sure, sometimes I worked long shifts or came home late if I was on a call, but she'd known that when we started dating. She never complained until we moved in together. She'd hurt me big time. I was ready to move on and leave this town, where I kept running into her and Thad everywhere I went.

When I went back to the gym after kicking her out, I found out she'd told some idiot gym rats we had an open relationship. Fuckers. How could those assholes screw her and then talk to me like nothing happened? I never told them we had an open relationship. Hell, I didn't know we had an open relationship. What the Fuck!

Not only did I lose the love of my life, or so I thought, but I had to find a new gym which sucked because that was the closest one to my house. I hadn't realized how easily I'd made it for her to have sex with those guys at my house, in our bed. Who knew? Not me, but most of them did by the looks they gave me after I threw her ass out. I guess they thought I was the stupid chump who went along with their secret trysts. Thank goodness I hadn't talked to my sergeant about a desk job.

Chugging the entire beer, while some dripped out of the sides of my mouth, I emptied the glass, and I held it up for everyone to see.

"I did it, you fuckers. Now stop egging me on!" I looked at all my buddies as they slapped me on the back, eliciting a long-ass, loud burp. "Sorry, ladies." Covering my mouth, I apologized to them. They were in the kitchen, and we were drinking on the patio, but the tri-panel sliding glass doors were wide open. I knew they heard my burp because while the men hooted and hollered, they giggled.

"Guys." I put my hand up to ward off the next beer George handed me. "No more. I have a four-hour drive tomorrow and I don't want to be hung over."

"I made you some coffee, Sean," Tori said from the kitchen island.

"Did you make some for me, too?" Alex winked at her on his way to the kitchen.

"I made a full pot for anyone who wants one." Tori kissed his cheek when Alex hugged her.

She was the sweetest one of them all, always thinking about her friend's welfare. George warned me she could get fiercely protective of Alex, even to the point of being mean, but I didn't believe him. I couldn't imagine a mean bone in Tori's body. Now Lizzy, her sister, was a spitfire like Maggie. He could definitely see either of those girls giving him shit. Although truth be told, Lizzy was calmer now that she was with George.

"Thank you, Tori, I'm headed your way." I slipped past the men, the low hum of their voices a background to the clatter of cutlery as I reached the kitchen, where the girls sat, legs swinging, on bar stools around the island.

"Here you go." Tori handed me a cup. "Add whatever you want."

"No need. I drink it black." I smiled at her.

"Hey." George grabbed my arm. "I want to talk to you before we all leave, since you're bringing the party down with coffee." George pulled me out to the patio.

"What's up?" I took a sip and sat on a patio chair.

"I saw you traded your minivan for a nice cherry red Mustang convertible."

"Yep, I wanted something different, something that didn't remind me of the van I bought for Kerri when we were talking about having kids. That van was always a painful reminder of our failed dreams." I looked out over Mark's huge sprawling lawn, wondering if he cut his grass because it would take hours or a riding lawnmower for all that acreage.

"I like the 'stang. It suits you." George sipped his coffee. "I wanted to thank you again for everything you did for me." George turned toward me.

"No need, man," I smiled. "It's what friends are for. Besides, you helped me out with the Kerri situation."

"I didn't do much." George shrugged.

"You listened and helped me get my head on straight. I was in a dangerous place after I found her with Thad." I mocked his name every time I said it.

"I only wish she hadn't fucked you over. I'm gonna miss you, but I get you need a change of pace. Who knows, maybe Lizzy and I will follow you up there?"

"No, you won't." I laughed and kicked George's foot with mine. "Your entire group of family and friends are here, but you can come visit."

"You're right. I love it here. We'll come and make sure you're doing well once you get settled in."

"You guys are welcome anytime." I grinned at George and watched all the guys come out with a cup of coffee. Points for the girls. I'm sure the men's change in drinks had something to do with them.

"Hey, are you guys done with your bro love moment?" Barrett smirked at them and sat in a chair.

Everyone else followed Barrett and filled in the empty chairs around the bonfire. While we reminisced about the fun times we'd had, the girls came out and sat on their respective partners' laps. Yep, it was time to go. My friends were all paired off and happy as shit. It was time for me to find my happily ever after.

# Chapter 2

# Haven Island

## Sean

I woke up to a beautiful Saturday morning. The sun was shining through the blinds into my bedroom since I had taken down and packed the blackout curtains I loved when I worked the night shift and slept during the day. The blinds helped dim the room, but slivers of light still pierced through, failing to fully blackout the room.

The only thing I was taking with me to Haven Island today was my suitcase filled with a week's worth of clothes and hygiene. George and Lizzy offered to pack up my kitchen and whatever else I hadn't finished. They also planned to meet the movers at my home on Saturday, as the movers would load the truck and drive straight to Haven Island. They planned to arrive at my new home around noon.

When Chief Alejandro Reyes from Haven Island PD called to offer me the job, I jumped at it. I was ready to get out of dodge. I gave my sergeant two-week's notice, but didn't think about going to Haven Island early and finding a place to live. Big mistake. I needed to find a place to live—an apartment or house—as soon as I got to Haven Island because I was starting my new job on Wednesday and couldn't afford to stay in a hotel for several weeks or months. What the hell was I thinking, giving myself only four days to find a place to live? Thankfully, the island was small, but that also meant there might not be much available. Clearly, I had high hopes and crazy ideas.

With Summer in high swing, I got lucky when the hotel on the beach, Ocean Breeze Resort, had a cancellation for a room facing the ocean. I booked it immediately for the entire week. Crossing my fingers that I'd find my new home before the movers arrived. The prospect of unwinding by the ocean, taking in the sights of women in bikinis, the scent of salt and coconut sunscreen, and the sounds of the waves, filled me with anticipation.

Excitement was building as I sat in my new convertible and took one last look at the small house I owned for the past five years. There were some wonderful memories in that house, especially the last two years with Kerri, but then she had to ruin it. Such a shame because it would've been a great starter home for us. With a shake of my head, I banished my gloomy thoughts and pulled out of the driveway as I listened to my engine rumbling to life. Time to think about new beginnings and leave the past where it belonged–in the past.

The drive to Haven Island wasn't too bad. I drove on the main highway north until my exit. Finding a gas station at that exit, I filled up with gas and put down the convertible top. I wanted to take in the entire island from the minute I drove onto it. When I interviewed with Chief Reyes, I'd done it all in a zoom call. The island's beauty and peace, as described by Chief Reyes, filled my thoughts; a vision of clear skies, white sand, and the rhythmic lull of the waves. I was ready for a change and loved Chief Reyes description of Haven Island. It was a lateral move, so the pay was the same, but I looked forward to a smaller community with less crime.

As I drove over the intracoastal bridge, the smell of salt and the feel of the wind in my hair eased my tension. The sun warming my face felt heavenly. Palm trees greeted me as soon as I crossed over the bridge. The island had one main road which branched out to several smaller roads and neighborhoods.

I noticed a rustic-looking restaurant called 'Hi Grill'. It was a weird name, but I was starving since I skipped breakfast. There had to be a story behind that name. Had someone been drunk or high when they came up with it? From the logo, it looked like they sold burgers and seafood. Two of my favorite foods. My stomach confirmed my hunger when it growled, reminding me I needed to eat and check out any local rental listings because once I checked into my hotel room, I might not leave. It would be nice to lie on the beach without a care in the world.

I pulled into one of several parking spots available. Maybe they got busier later? I closed the convertible top, got out, and locked my car to prevent anyone from stealing it. I knew from my conversations with the captain that crime was low, but I wasn't taking any chances on my first day in town. The captain might love his town and be wearing rose-colored glasses.

The hostess escorted me to a booth by the front window and handed me a menu. Perfect. I could look outside and keep an eye out for my car, the traffic, and anyone who entered the restaurant.

"Cassie, will be right with you."

"Thank you," I smiled and looked over the menu, excited to see lots of fish options. Back home, I ate a lot of fish, but on an island it might be fresher. The grilled fish sandwich looked good.

"Hi, I'm Cassie. Can I get you something to drink?"

I looked up and gazed at the most exotically beautiful, brown doe-eyed woman I'd ever seen. The long brown hair, loosely gathered in a messy ponytail, had a few wispy tendrils that gently caressed her cheeks.

"Hi, Cassie. I'm Sean."

Cassie frowned. "You must be new in town. I've never seen you before."

"And you know everyone in town," I smirked. She was sassy and observant. Two of my favorite qualities.

"Yep." Cassie's lips popped out the 'p'. "I work two jobs—one in the morning and one in the afternoon to evening—so I pretty much see everyone during the day."

"Where else do you work?"

"Why do you want to know?" Cassie tilted her head and popped her gum.

"I just got hired by Haven Island PD and I'm ready to meet all my new neighbors." I grinned, trying to ease her into a conversation.

"Hi PD, huh," Cassie smirked. "I guess I'll see more of you in the mornings."

My grin widened. Was she coming onto me? "What do you mean?"

"Not what your dirty mind is thinking." Cassie pointed her pen at me. "My second job is at the coffee shop and all the cops come in for coffee, usually in the morning, but some throughout the day."

"Sorry." Holding up my hands, I chuckled. "I wasn't trying to offend you. I love my morning cup of coffee, so I'm sure I'll see you there next week before I report for duty."

"Our coffee is the best way to start your day." Cassie placed her pen on her pad, ready to write my order. "Are you ready to order?"

"Yes, but quick question. Why is this place called Hi Grill?"

"Hi for Haven Island, all the locals shorten the name of the island to hi…," Cassie rolled her eyes at him like he was an idiot, and she was saying duh, "and Grill because we grill all our main entrees. Everything is homemade by our resident chef, Carl."

"Got it." I nodded. It made sense, especially now that he remembered her saying Hi PD instead of HIPD.

"So, what'll you have? I don't have all day." Cassie cocked her hip and blew a bubble.

Scanning the nearly empty restaurant, I only saw two other occupied tables. One by a couple sipping coffee and the other by a lone, pretty female engrossed in a book.

She acted more like a waitress in a big city than a beach town. Where was her southern hospitality? Which caused me to wonder if she was from here or a transplant like me.

"I'll have a glass of water and the grilled fish sandwich with veggies on the side." I handed her my menu.

"You're one of those, huh?"

"One of who?" I squinted at her. What was she talking about?

"A health nut."

"I do watch what I eat. I take it you don't."

Cassie pointed to her hips. "Do these hips look like I eat healthy all the time?"

"I think your hips look great." The words slipped out of my mouth before I could sensor them. But, hell, she was perfect with curves in the right places.

"I see you're a health nut and a sweet talker. The girls will love you around here." Cassie took the menu.

"What about you?" I quirked my eyebrow at her. As the saying goes, in for a penny, in for a pound. Cassie opened her mouth to respond, but something outside caught her attention. She squinted and moved to the right as if looking for something. Or was it someone?

I glanced out the window, but all I saw were the cars parked in front of the restaurant, including mine. "Are you okay?"

"Uh, yeah. Sorry," Cassie blinked and faced me. "What were you saying?"

"Nothing, it's all good." I watched Cassie continue to turn around and stare outside as she walked away from my table. I wondered what she saw to put that puzzled look on her face.

Chapter 3

# Hottie at Table 6

## Cassie

Was that Elias from the coffee shop? Did he hide behind the van? I stepped to the right to get a better view, but I couldn't see him anymore. Elias came to our coffee shop like clockwork every morning. We got a lot of regulars, but Elias by far was the creepiest whenever he stared at me with his blank eyes. He asked me out once, but I turned him down. I could see his anger rising, but he never said a word. Although, I could feel his stare boring into me the entire time I made his coffee. Despite everything, he showed up every day, but didn't ask again. Some days he sat at a table to drink his coffee and others he would take it to go, but I'd never seen him at the restaurant. Anyway, maybe my eyes were playing tricks on me and it wasn't him at all.

The hottie at table six was a serious distraction. My customer service skills were impeccable, but something about him made me nervous and my sassiness came out. I usually reserved that attitude for my friends, not new customers. I bet he looked even hotter when he had his HIPD uniform on. Something I was bound to see sooner rather than later if he held up his promise to come in for coffee next week. I couldn't wait. I loved seeing a man in uniform and truly enjoyed talking to the officers when they came in for coffee or a breakfast sandwich and flirted with me. It was innocent flirting because I knew most of them since they were in diapers.

Haven Island was a small town where everyone knew everyone. I've lived here all my life and enjoyed working at the coffee shop for my mom, Judy, and the restaurant for my dad, Carl. You'd think one family running two businesses would be stressful, but they made it work. The coffee shop, Hi Café, was open from 6:00am to 2:00pm and Hi Grill was open from 11:00am to 8:00pm. My mom usually left the coffee shop at eleven to help dad and either my sister or I would alternate going with her if the coffee shop was slow or after we closed.

Today, the coffee shop was slow, and it was my day to come to the restaurant. I loved working both jobs but enjoyed the coffee shop more. Unfortunately, so did my sister, Katie. So, we compromised and alternated days at the restaurant. With the restaurant slow today, Katie had the day off to enjoy the beautiful sunny weather at the beach. That's what had me so grumpy. I loved a good day at the beach. Lying on the sand and letting the sun's rays tan my skin as I listened to the waves crashing on the shore and smelled the salt in the air. I loved everything about Haven Island.

When I went to college, on the mainland, to get my business degree, I came home every weekend and hightailed it back to the island right after graduation. Being the oldest Fulton child, I knew I would eventually take over one of the businesses. My parents, feeling the effects of age and reduced energy, often hinted that I should inherit one of their companies so they could enjoy their later in life years. I hoped it was the coffee shop, but the restaurant took more of their time. Then again, they loved working at the restaurant more than the coffee shop because they got to spend their days together. I loved the rustic beachy look of the restaurant, but I would love to add an outdoor bar with extra seating so guests could enjoy the fresh outdoors.

"Cassie, foods up." The brass counter bell, a familiar sound in the restaurant, dinged as my father signaled me. I hated that sound. If I were in charge, that bell would be the first thing to go. I complained to my dad, whining about the sound, but he simply stated that it served its purpose in snapping me out of my daydreams.

"Thanks," I smiled and grabbed the plate. I supposed he was right.

I delivered Sean his water earlier, but didn't say a word to him when he thanked me. He made me nervous, and I didn't want to fall for another outsider that came by thinking they wanted to be an officer on the island, but after not being a part of too much action, left. I had been hurt before, and I was unwilling to become too attached or invested in him if he proved to be another short-timer.

"Here you go." I quickly placed the plate in front of him and was ready to leave when he reached for my hand. A jolt of electricity raced up my arm, shocking my senses. Immediately pulling my hand away, I rubbed it, staring at him wide-eyed. I'd never felt such an instant attraction to a man. From the look on his face, if I was a betting woman, I'd put money on him feeling the same way. His frowning gaze bounced between my hand and his.

"Uh, thanks." Sean pointed to the seat opposite him in the booth. "Can you sit for a minute?"

"Why?"

"You're a local, and I would love to have your opinion."

I hesitated because I wasn't sure sitting with him was such a good idea. I mean, I wanted to, but didn't want to get too far into him.

"Please." Sean added, and I caved.

"Sure, why not? It's not too busy in here right now." I slid into the booth. "What do you want my opinion on?"

"I'm staying at the Ocean Breeze Resort, but I want to find a place to buy. If nothing's available, I'll rent until a suitable property becomes available. Can I show you my options? Get your opinion of the places?" Sean handed me his phone. "I've put everything in a .pdf file so all you have to do is scroll up to see them all."

"Wow." I took his phone and stared at him." You're anally organized."

"Gee, thanks." Sean rubbed the back of his neck.

"Sorry, I didn't mean that as an insult. It's a compliment, really. Most people on the island have a relaxed and disorganized approach to life. I'm not used to someone being this together." I pointed at his phone in my hand.

Scrolling through, I saw he had several houses in the northern part of the island near the docks and some on the southern end, near the park. I recognized all the houses he had in his document. Sliding out of my seat, I stood next to him. He looked up at me, confusion written all over his face.

"Slide over."

Sean smiled and scooted so I could sit next to him. I pushed his food in front of him and placed the phone between us on the table.

"Eat while we talk. Do you have a boat?" I asked when Sean grabbed his sandwich.

"No, no boat." Sean took a bite.

"Okay, well, these up here are more expensive because they are near the marina and most people who live there have boats. So, if you are looking for a less expensive option, you might want to buy one of these." I scrolled down until I found what I was looking for. "These are near the park. They're actually right across the street." I pointed out the window.

Sean looked over and nodded while he chewed. "Do you recognize any of them?"

"I know all of them." I scrolled to one house near the park. "This one is owned by widow Mary. Her husband Larry passed away a few months ago and her daughter wants her to move in with her on the mainland. Plus, it's the house where she raised her kids and is too big for just her now. Larry always kept the house and yard pristine. The beach and a wooded side yard with a path to the park provide privacy. It is pricier than the other ones in that area, but it's absolutely beautiful inside and out."

"Sounds like the first place I want to look at. I'll call the realtor." Sean picked up his phone and dialed the number. "Hi, I pulled your listing from your website and would love to see the house on Island Lane. Yes, I want to buy not rent. Yes, I can be there in an hour. Thank you. See you then."

"You will love that house. This other one is nice, too." I pointed to a much smaller house in the marina area with a higher price. "It's more because of the location, but it's a great house."

I kept pointing out several houses while he ate, and Sean called the realtors to schedule appointments. Some houses used the same realtors, which made it easier for him. After eating, Sean's schedule included four house visits—two today and two tomorrow.

"Well, my work is done." I slid over and stood.

Sean wiped his mouth. "Cassie, would you mind going with me to check out these houses? I could use another opinion, and I don't know anyone in town."

"I can't. I'm scheduled to work here until closing, and I work at the coffee shop in the morning." I would've loved to go looking at homes and seeing their interior decor, but I couldn't leave my family hanging.

"Hi, I'm Cassie's mom, Judy."

Sean wiped his hands and mouth before extending his hand. "It's nice to meet you, ma'am. I love your food and restaurant."

"Thank you. What's your name?" Judy shook his hand and smiled.

"My name's Sean O'Reilly. I just moved here from South Florida and I'm starting my new job with Haven Island PD on Monday. I was looking for a house and asked Cassie for her opinion. I didn't get her in trouble for sitting with me, did I?"

"No." Judy shook her head. "It's slow right now. It usually picks up around four thirty for our early bird specials. Cassie, you can go, but please be back around five."

"Are you sure, mom?" Did I really want to go house shopping with Sean? Was this a bad idea and my mom was jumping on the Sean bandwagon because she wanted me married and with child? A girl could get wrapped up in a hot guy and a beautiful house.

"Yes, go. We'll be fine, and I'm sure this young man could use your help."

"Thank you, ma'am." Sean pulled out his wallet and left enough cash for the bill and his tip.

Ugh, he was racking up points with me and my mom. We all loved a good tipper. He was hot with his sandy brown wavy hair falling over his forehead, gorgeous baby blue eyes, organized, polite, charmer, good tipper, and math smart. How could I say no to all that when my body was already reacting to him?

"You kids go and have fun. Give me your apron." Mom reached behind me and undid the knot, pulling it away. "I'll see you back here at five." Then she shooed us out of the restaurant.

From behind Sean's back, I glared at my mother. I wanted her to know I was onto her matchmaking scheme. Though I adored my mother and understood her desire for grandchildren, her attempts to set me up had to stop. As a grown woman, I chose my own dates. She was getting out of control. Besides, didn't most moms not want their daughters to get in cars with strangers? What had gotten into her, anyway?

## Chapter 4

# She is So Beautiful

## Elias

What the hell was she doing? She never talks to me like she was with that guy. He must be new in town because I've never seen him before and I watch everyone. I'm a freelance photographer and I love to take photos of people and places. My work has never been published, but that's only because people lack the discernment to recognize true photographic excellence.

I need to move here so I can watch her closely. Living with Mother on the mainland is not convenient if we are going to date. Although I could just move in with her. She has her own room in her parents' house. I'm sure they wouldn't mind us staying in her room. At least until we find an apartment to rent.

She is mine.

Shit, did she just sit next to that loser in the booth? What the hell, Cassie? That is not something my girlfriend should be doing. He might get the wrong impression. I'll go to my car and wait for her to get off work so I can talk to her. She needs to understand that she shouldn't be talking to other men like that.

I forgive her in the mornings when she flirts with the cops, only because she is on the other side of the counter and needs to be nice to them as a business owner. But I draw the line at her sitting next to another man. She needs to learn her rightful place if we are going to be together. Mother wouldn't like for a girl to treat me this way.

I turned to go to my car when I saw her get up and leave with the guy. They were getting into his car. She should not be leaving with a stranger. Didn't she know she was not safe? I will follow them and see where they go, but I need to keep my distance. The last thing I need is to get into a fight in public.

I'll talk to her tonight, and I will teach her how disrespectful she was to me today, but first, let me call Mother and let her know her lunch will be late.

# Chapter 5

# Widow Mary's House

## Sean

My day was getting better and better now that I had a beautiful woman sitting in my hot rod with the top down. It was a picture-perfect moment.

"Do you want some sunglasses?" I put mine on and pointed to my glove compartment. "I have an extra pair in there."

"Sure, thanks." Cassie grabbed them and put them on. "Are these for all the girls you let sit in your car?"

"Nope, they're actually my sisters. She left them in my car when I bought it."

"You went car shopping with your sister? Impressive." Cassie buckled in.

"She has excellent taste for a teenager." I entered the address on my GPS before pulling out. "Besides, I wanted to spend more time with her before I left." I loved my sister even though she was entering her bratty years.

"How old is she?"

"Thirteen going on Thirty."

"How old are you?" Cassie smirked.

"Just turned forty. Why?"

"That's a huge age gap."

"Yeah, I lost my mom a few years back, and the grief was still raw when my dad brought his new wife home, not even a year after the funeral. He swore up and down that he didn't cheat on my mom, insisting that meeting Cheryl was a thoughtful gift from mom in heaven since she knew he hated living alone. It was difficult to accept her as my stepmom because she's only slightly older than me. Having a baby was her wish. I can't imagine life without my sister, Lynn."

"Do you get along with your family now?" Cassie leaned her elbow on the door with her hand on the top of the front windshield.

"I do. Dad and I aren't super close, but I love my little sister. It's not her fault her father is retirement age, and her mom doesn't have a lot of time for her."

"So, you don't like your stepmom?"

"Nah, Cheryl is fine. We get along in small doses. I just wish she spent more time loving her daughter and my father than spending his money with her friends."

I was going the speed limit, 35mph, but the ocean breeze was blowing her ponytail and more strands of her hair around her face. I should've asked her if she was okay with the top down.

"Sorry, do you want me to pull over and put the top up?" I glanced her way.

"Nope, I love feeling the wind on my face." Cassie closed her eyes and smiled.

A girl after my heart. Kerri had hated having the top down when I owned the convertible corvette. She always complained about how it made her hot and messed up her hair. She wanted a minivan to fit all the kids we were going to have. I even took her to the dealership to pick it out. Yet another reason for selling that fucking minivan and going back to a convertible, just not a corvette.

"Me too. I had a minivan for a while and really missed the freedom of a convertible." We were already at widow Mary's house near the park. It was beautiful. A two-story home with a garage. The perfectly landscaped lawn, vibrant with hibiscus and orchids, led up to a welcoming front porch, complete with a swing and a couple of rocking chairs.

"Wait." Cassie grabbed my arm when I turned off the car. "You drove a minivan? Do you have kids? Are you married?" Cassie looked appalled.

"Yes...no...and no." I grabbed her hand when she tried to pull away after hearing my first yes. I needed to explain what I meant because with her mouth open and anger shining in her eyes, she was about to bolt if I was reading her right. "Yes, I drove a minivan, but no, I don't have kids, and I'm not married."

"Hellooo!" The realtor waved from the front porch.

"Can we talk about this later?" I whispered and squeezed her hand. "I promise you, I'm very single."

"Sure, yeah." Cassie pulled her hand away and got out.

I left the top down and locked the car. Seemed like a silly thing to do with the top down, but it was a force of habit. I caught up to Cassie and placed my left hand on her lower back.

"Hi, I'm Sean and this is Cassie." I extended my right hand out to shake the realtor's hand.

"Hi, Sean. I'm Josie Hale." Josie shook my hand. "Hey, Cassie. How are you?"

"I'm good Josie, how are you?" Cassie hugged Josie.

"So, you two know each other?" I pointed between the two of them.

"Yep, Josie and I went to school together. How's the realty business going?"

"It's going. I'm still not selling enough to stop working at the hotel, but I'm getting there." Josie turned and opened the door. "Come on in."

"So, you work two jobs, too?" I guided Cassie inside before me.

"Most people around here do double duty because some places are busier than others during our seasonal times."

"Wow, this place is just like I remembered it." Cassie's face lit up like a child at Christmas as she looked around on her walk down the hallway to the back sliding glass door. "Look at that view!"

I followed Cassie through the house. She was right. The view was breathtaking. How the hell was a house with this view on my budget? I turned to Josie, who was showing us two houses today. "Does the other house you have to show me have a view like this?"

"No," Josie sighed. "This house is special. Mary just listed it yesterday after a lot of pressure from her daughter. I guarantee you it will sell quickly and likely start a bidding war."

"What if I pay cash?"

"You're a cop. How can you have that much money?" Cassie faced him with her arms crossed.

"I'm forty and have done well in the stock market. Does that meet your approval?"

I watched her cheeks go pink before she lowered her head and mumbled, "Hot, smart, and loaded. Shit."

I smiled, glad I'd made an impression on her because she definitely had my insides all twisted up.

"Come on, let's check out the rest of the house." I led Cassie away from the living room. "Josie, lead the way."

Josie took them upstairs to look at the three bedrooms and two bathrooms upstairs. Two rooms shared a jack and jill bathroom, while the other had its own bathroom. It looked like a small main bedroom. Josie explained it was the master bedroom until Mary and Todd added a new one downstairs a few years ago. The laundry room was downstairs next to the garage door, and the remodeled kitchen now had an open concept design flowing into the living room and included a breakfast nook. The new master bedroom behind the garage had bay windows and a door leading out to the beach.

The door swung open, revealing a small patch of emerald green grass, the warm sand beckoning me towards the breathtaking turquoise water. "Wow, this is stunning."

Cassie slipped off her shoes and tugged my hand. "Come on."

Her excitement was so contagious; I flung off my boat shoes as she pulled me along. With the salty air filling my lungs, I followed her into the ocean up to my shins. The water felt cooler than in South Florida, more refreshing. Cassie went deeper and bent down to splash water up around us.

"Isn't this beautiful?"

"It sure is." I knew Cassie meant the ocean, but I meant her. Watching the expression of joy on her face as she played in the crystal-clear blue water was abso-fucking-lutely beautiful. I could imagine playing with her in the ocean every day of my life. I turned around and saw Josie standing on the patio, smiling at us, before she took a call.

"I knew you would love this place." Cassie's voice turned me back around to face her. "I can still go with you to see the other place, but you won't find a nicer place than this one if you can afford it."

"I can afford it." I stepped further into the cool water, grabbed Cassie holding her tightly against my chest, and whispered, "thank you for making me see this place first."

"I'm glad you like it." Cassie stepped back and glanced down.

My hug must've embarrassed her from the way she pulled away from me and wouldn't look me in the eye. I needed to go slower and convince her I wasn't just out for a quick fuck. I put my arm around her shoulders and led her back onto the porch. "Come on, let's talk to Josie about my offer."

"There's a spicket over there so we can wash our feet." Cassie pointed to the left of the bedroom door.

I followed her and turned it on, washing the sand off before putting our shoes back on.

"Here are some paper towels so you can dry your legs and feet." Josie held the roll out to them. "So, do you want to make Mary an offer? That was her daughter on the phone."

"We do." I felt Cassie's body stiffen under my arm. Shit, I'd said we. "I mean, I do."

If I didn't start watching what I said, Cassie was going to run.

"Are you guys dating?" Josie clapped her hands. "I'm so happy for you, Cassie."

# Damn that Man and His Charming Smile

## Cassie

"No." My eyes bugged out, and I shrugged his arm off my shoulders. "We just met. I'm just helping him."

"We did just meet." Sean faced me and grasped my hand. "But I was hoping you would go out with me."

"I'll give you two a minute." Josie hightailed it inside while I stared at Sean.

After an awkward silence, I slipped my hand out of Sean's and bent down to dry my feet so I could put my shoes on. I needed to take a step back because I didn't want to get in too deep. He was so easy to fall for.

"I..I have to get back to work." I grabbed the handle on the sliding glass door.

"Cassie, wait." Sean placed his hand over mine. "Will you go out with me? We can get dinner tomorrow or any night this week. It can be casual."

The thrill of a new romance and my apprehension battled within me. Who knows? He might love it here and become a permanent resident. Didn't I at least owe it to him and me to try? Decision made, I would get his number and then think about calling him.

"Give me your number and I'll call you." I handed him my phone.

Sean put his number in and sent himself a quick text.

"Did you just text yourself from my phone?" I took my phone back. Now he had my number, and I was no longer in the driver's seat.

"I did," Sean grinned.

I rolled my eyes at him and entered the house. We needed to move on so I could get to work.

"So, what do you think?" Josie called out from the kitchen. "Do you want to put a bid in?"

"I do. Please tell Mary and her daughter that I'm willing to pay their full asking price. I can give them half in cash tomorrow, and I'll finance the rest."

"That sounds great. Do you want to see the next house?"

"Nope. Can you call her now, because if she accepts my offer, then I'm done house hunting."

"Okay. I'll be right back." Josie pulled out her phone and stepped outside to make her call.

I spun around and stared at him, dumbfounded. "You're gonna buy the first house you saw?"

"Why not? It's beautiful, and you said it was the best one for the price and location. I trust you."

"You don't even know me." Had he lost his mind?

"I know you love your family. Your parents own two thriving establishments. You work yourself to the bone between the two jobs, and you're nice to your friends. What else do I need to know?" Sean shrugged.

"Uh, I don't know. Maybe I kill my ex-boyfriends or I'm a fugitive running from the law."

Sean burst out laughing and pointed at her. "That's the funniest thing you've said since we met."

"Why? I could have a mean streak?"

"Okay, okay," Sean held his hand out and controlled his laughter. "Show me your mean face."

I looked at him like I would an irate customer.

"Now that's just adorable." Sean chuckled.

His reaction made me so angry; I shot him the meanest glare I could muster.

"Okay." Sean wiped the smile off his face and pointed at her, dropping the smirk off his face. "I don't like that face at all. That face means I'm in the doghouse and we haven't even gone on our first date."

"Hey, great news." Josie came back in smiling until she saw my face. "Cassie, are you okay?"

"I'm fine. I was showing Sean my mean face." I forced a similar fake smile I use for difficult customers, one that never fully reaches my eyes.

"Oh." Josie pretended to shiver. "I've seen that face. It's the one she wore when she caught her high school boyfriend kissing another girl under the bleachers. Not only did the girl end up with a black eye, but the boy was our quarterback, and he had to sit out that night's game for a groin injury."

Sean cocked his eyebrow and stared at me. "Now this story I need to hear."

"Thanks, Josie. Wait until you meet a guy you like, so I can air out your dirty laundry." I turned to Sean. "He deserved it for putting his lips on another girl while dating me."

"You like me." Sean smiled broadly, placed his hands in his pockets, and rocked back and forth.

"That's all you got from my story?" Just like a guy to not catch the violent act that my jealousy caused, and to focus on his ego.

"That's all I care about." Sean shrugged.

"Whatever," I huffed and looked at Josie. "What was your good news?"

"Mary and her daughter accepted your offer." Josie raised her arms in celebration. "Congratulations on your new home!"

"Thank you." Sean extended his hand. "How soon can we close? When can I move in? I have a moving truck coming next Saturday with all my stuff."

"I'll set up the closing with the bank, but I'm sure I can do it this week since you and Mary's daughter want this to happen quickly. I'll cancel the next appointment and text you the info as soon as I can."

Sean's hand on my lower back guided me out the door as Josie locked up. His touch sent shivers down to my toes, a delightful tingling sensation spreading through me.

"That sounds great. Thanks again, Josie."

"My pleasure. We'll talk soon." Josie turned and hugged me. "It's good to see you, Cassie. We need to get together and do lunch or go out for drinks."

"I'd like that." I stumbled backward, colliding with Sean, who instantly put his arm around my waist, pulling me close.

"See you guys later," Josie winked at us and left.

Sean and I both waved back before I pulled out of his embrace, heading toward his car. "Can you drive me back to the restaurant, please? My parents could use my help."

Sean strolled to his car and opened the door for me. After he shut my door and went around the front to get in, he checked his watch. "How about a celebratory drink at the hotel bar? It's close to the restaurant, and I need to go check in."

How could I turn down his puppy dog look? "Sure, why not? But just one drink."

"Of course." Sean smiled and drove them to the hotel.

Damn. That man's smile could charm the pants off any woman. I followed Sean into the lobby and waited next to him while he checked in, and the young girl behind the lobby desk checked him out. Oh my God, she was so obvious. Didn't she realize I was standing right there? I was so angry. If I were a cartoon character, the girl behind the counter would've seen the steam coming out of my ears.

"Oh, hey." Josie stepped out from an office door behind the stupid flirty girl.

Sean tapped the counter. "Is this the hotel where you work?"

"Yep, I work here in the evenings." Josie smiled at Sean before she glanced at me. She knew my angry face well. Grinning, she put her arm around the young girl and said, "Jenny, I'll finish his reservation."

"But I'm almost done, Josie."

"I know. And you've done a good job, but I know Mr. O'Reilly and Ms. Fulton."

"Oh, are they together?" Jenny glanced at all of them.

"No." Sean said at the same time, I said "Yes".

Sean glanced over his shoulder at me, and I glared back. Not knowing why, I was agreeing to be with him when I kept delaying our date. But my stomach was in knots at the thought of him with another girl.

"Uh, yes." Sean reached back and wrapped his arm around my back, pulling me against his side. "We are together, right, honey?"

Sean's fingers gently tilted my face upward, his thumb brushing my cheek as he leaned down to kiss me. His sudden move made me gasp, allowing him to explore every corner of my mouth. His tongue, hot and slick, moved sensuously into my mouth, stealing my breath away. Time seemed to stop as the kiss lasted several minutes, an eternity of stolen moments, before a throat clearing broke the spell, reminding us we were still standing at the hotel's lobby desk.

Suddenly, I snapped out of my daze and quickly withdrew. Before turning to Josie, Sean leaned in and gave me a fleeting, tender kiss. That's when I noticed the young girl was gone, leaving only Josie behind the desk. Her grin stretching from ear to ear, a mischievous glint in her eyes.

"Here are your keys," Josie said, handing Sean a small key folder with the logo on it. "I gave you two, just in case." Josie winked at me. "Written inside are the room number, Wi-Fi, and password. Do you need a luggage cart?"

"No, I only have my suitcase. But my girlfriend and I...," Sean smiled and kissed my temple, "are going to the hotel bar for a drink first. I'll bring my bag in later."

"You are insufferable." I groaned. I had created a monster now that I had given him the impression that we were dating. Aw, hell.

"Hey, you said you were with me. I'm just letting your friend know where we'll be in case you turn into a serial killer, and I'm never seen again." Sean shrugged.

"Funny." Cassie shoved him playfully. "Not."

Josie grinned. "If there is anything else I can do for you, let me know? I'm here until ten."

"Thanks, Josie. I appreciate all your help."

"No problem."

"Come on, honey, let's go get that drink." Sean wiggled his eyebrows and grabbed my hand, pulling me toward the indoor bar.

On the outside, I acted put out, but deep down, I loved our easy banter. I'd never had that with anyone before. He made dating as easy as breathing. Letting my walls drop, I looked forward to getting to know him better.

Chapter 7

# I Don't Want This Date to End

## Sean

"What do you want to drink?" I led Cassie to a nearby high-top table for two near the bar.

"I'll have a virgin Piña Colada. I don't drink much, and no one wants to be served dinner by a drunk waitress."

"Valid point." I nodded. "I'll be right back."

I walked up to the bar, got the bartender's attention, and placed our drink order. Leaning against the bar, I turned around and looked between Cassie and the guests milling around the lobby. The guests' excitement was palpable, their laughter and chatter filling the air. It was heartwarming to see the romantic couples stealing kisses, the boundless energy of children as they played, their parents' laughter mixing with their joyous shrieks. Their smiles were contagious. The bartender interrupted my thoughts.

"Here you go, man." The bartender slid the drinks in front of me. "Do you want to open a tab?"

"Not this time, but thanks."

"Give me a second and I'll give you your bill."

"Sure, I'm gonna give my girl her drink. I'll be back."

Placing the drink in front of Cassie, I said, "A virgin Piña Colada for my beautiful girlfriend, so you don't get drunk and spill any drinks or food on your customers tonight. I'll be back in a minute."

After paying and tipping the bartender, I came back to Cassie and raised my glass for a toast. Cassie raised hers and stayed quiet.

"To our new house and great tips for you today at work. Cheers." I tapped her glass and drank.

"You mean your new house?" Cassie squinted at me.

"That's what I said," I grinned. "My new house."

Shit, a slip of the tongue was going to get me in trouble.

Cassie took a drink before she set her drink down. "Thanks for the tips, part of the toast. Some people don't tip anymore, so any amount I get, I put away for my future nest egg."

Whew, she was ignoring my comment and moving on—good idea to change the topic.

"What are you going to use your nest egg money on?"

"I want to travel." Cassie shrugged. "Not anywhere crazy, just in the United States. With so much to see in the States, an RV road trip is high on my list."

"Which States?" I asked between sips. Travelling around the U.S. would be fun.

"All fifty states are on my bucket list," she grinned.

"All fifty?" I cocked an eyebrow. "Wow, have you been to any of them other than Florida?"

"No, but the first ones on my bucket list are Washington, D.C., New York, and Montana. Have you been to any of them?" Cassie sat back, a dreamy look in her eyes as she happily sipped her virgin drink.

I would do anything to keep that look on her face. "I've been to D.C. and New York, but never Montana. I've heard Big Sky Country is quite beautiful." My friend Mark always talked about the beauty of Montana. I crossed my arms and leaned them on the table, watching her.

"You have friends in Montana?"

"Not exactly." I smiled. "My friend Mark was from Montana and his family still has a ranch there."

"Ooh," her eyes widened. "Is it a working ranch? I've always wanted to visit a real ranch."

I chuckled because, having heard the stories about Mark's family ranch; it sounded exactly like what Cassie would like to experience. "It is. They have horses and raise cattle."

"That must be so cool."

"I'm in." I blurted.

"What?" Cassie shook her head. "You're in what?"

"Whatever put that sexy, dreamy look in your eyes," I reached for her hand and laid our intertwined hands on the table between us, "I'm in. I'll make it happen. Just say the word."

Cassie finished her drink. "I...I need to get back to work."

"You got it." I finished my drink and drove her to the restaurant. Cassie was quiet on the drive and I let her be, but only so I could let her relax before I asked for a date.

When we arrived at our destination, I reached for Cassie's hand when she unbuckled her seat. "So, can we have our second date this week?"

"What happened to our first date?" Cassie froze and stared at me.

"The drinks we just shared could be our first date." I gently pulled her hand up to my lips. Her soft skin felt amazing against my lips as I kissed the back of her hand. "Are you working tomorrow?"

"No, it's my day off, believe it or not. I was planning to go to the beach."

"Now that I don't have to go house shopping, my day is free. Will you join me at the beach?"

My grip tightened as she attempted to pull her hand away. I felt the slight tremor in her fingers as her hesitance became clear. I held my breath, unwilling to release it until she answered. The silence was thick with unspoken words as she considered my proposition, and I could feel the tension radiating from her.

"As friends?" Cassie stared down at our hands.

"I think you know I like you more than a friend, and I'm pretty sure you feel the same way." Placing my pointer finger under her chin, I lifted her face. I could tell a lot by looking into someone's eyes, and right now I wanted to see her truth. "Am I wrong?"

"No." The corner of Cassie's lips twitched. "You're not wrong."

"Why won't you give me a shot? Who hurt you?"

"It wasn't one person. Several ex-boyfriends had sworn they'd weather the island life with me, promising a future together, but months later, after I confessed my love, their resolve crumbled. Overwhelmed by a longing for the vibrant city life they'd either left behind or wanted to experience, they urged me to return with them. But I couldn't. They couldn't understand the profound connection between my family, this island, and my very soul. It's a bond as deep as the ocean surrounding us. The vibrant pulse of Haven Island flows through my veins." Cassie's eyes watered.

"Did you explain that to them?" Wow, he'd never heard such intense emotion in someone's voice as they spoke about their home.

"I did," Cassie admitted, her head bowed, "but they still left me."

I used my thumb to catch the tear running down her face. "Well, I'm staying. Hell, I just bought a house."

"Some of them had houses, too," Cassie mumbled.

"I'm so sorry that happened to you, but I'm not going to do that to you. Please don't lump me into their shitty ass category. My new job starts on Wednesday, and I'm not going anywhere." Letting go of her hand, I caressed her cheek with my thumb. "Please, give us a chance." I leaned in slowly and softly kissed her lips.

"Okay," Cassie whispered, licked her lips, and nodded. "Please, don't hurt me."

"I'm not perfect, Cass. I'm sure I'll make stupid mistakes, but what I can promise you is that I never want to do anything that causes you pain. Will you please meet me at the hotel beach tomorrow?"

Cassie whispered, "Okay."

I smiled and gave her another sweet kiss. "Come by around eleven. I'll even feed you in the outdoor restaurant before we lie on the beach and relax." I tilted my head toward the restaurant. "I think you better go in. Your mom's staring at us."

"That's her happy look." Cassie pointed at her, and Judy scurried away from the window. "She likes you. But be careful. She's probably planning our wedding as we sit here." Cassie rolled her eyes and opened the door.

I busted out laughing. "So, I'll see you tomorrow at eleven?"

"Yes." Cassie shut the door, smiling.

I waited until she disappeared inside the bustling restaurant, the sounds of chatter fading as the door closed behind her. I returned her wave one last time before driving off. Back at the hotel, I ordered room service—a delicious steak—looking forward to a relaxing evening watching TV in my plush, comfortable room.

Chapter 8

# Fulton's Inquisition

## Cassie

I braced myself for all the questions my parents were going to throw at me as I went into the kitchen to get my apron.

"So." my mom followed. "How did it go?"

"It was good. We went to see the widow Mary's house. He fell in love with it, put in an offer, and Mary and her daughter accepted it." I tied the apron around my waist. "He closes this week."

"That's great. It's a beautiful home. I didn't realize Mary was leaving. I guess her daughter finally convinced her. Who's the realtor?" Mom grabbed the plates dad placed on the counter.

"Who is this mystery guy you ladies are talking about?" Dad began cooking another filet of fish.

"The realtor is Josie, and the guy is Sean." I grabbed a pad to get some orders and glared at my dad. "Don't pretend mom didn't already give you a full description of Sean, especially since he was in here earlier today."

"She did, but I'd like to hear how you feel about him." Dad flipped the fish on the grill.

"That house sale will really help Josie," Judy said after she delivered the dishes and came back into the kitchen.

"Yeah, she wants her realty business to take off so she can go down to just one job. I told her we'd get together soon."

"You girls should. It would be fun." Her mom hip bumped her. "You guys used to hang out together all the time before you both started working two jobs. You need to learn to multitask. I work a lot too, but I always find the time to get coffee or lunch with my friends."

Mom always loved the girls I hung out with, probably because she was best friends with their moms. My besties and I were inseparable, spending countless hours together in dance and cheerleading throughout school. Mom always taught me you need girlfriends, not just boyfriends.

"Little girl." Her father pointed his spatula in her direction. "You didn't answer my question."

"I like him, but I'm afraid of liking him too much. What if he leaves?"

"I understand, but at some point, you gotta give someone a shot." Dad shrugged. "Your mom said he seems nice."

"He is nice." I placed the pad in my apron pocket. "And he's gonna start working with the Hi PD."

"And," –her mom's embrace, a jarring side hug, squeezed the air from her lungs– "he just bought a house. I agree with your dad. You need to give him a chance. If you want to be married someday and have a family, you're gonna have to open yourself up sometime."

"Okay." I kissed my mom on her cheek. "I give in. I don't have the energy to argue with you, Sean, and dad."

"Ooh, so he wants to date you, too." Her mom smiled. "I'm happy for you, honey. Enjoy the ride."

"Thanks, mom."

"Okay, enough mushy stuff." Dad finished the fish sandwich he was working on and waved his spatula in a circular motion above his head. "Everybody, get back to work. We have customers to feed."

As I was leaving the kitchen, I saw mom toss a piece of broccoli at my dad, which he caught in his mouth. My parents were always goofing off. It was one of several reasons, including shared values and mutual respect, why they could live and work together harmoniously. She hoped to find a relationship as warm and playful as the one they shared, full of inside jokes and happy memories.

I had several tables to tend to, which were filled with a hodgepodge of customers. Some were locals and others were tourists. Luckily or thanks to Sean's toast, they were all tipping well. I spent my entire shift thinking about Sean. Being with him felt so natural, and I could imagine the rest of my life with him in that beautiful house.

The front door jingled, and I saw Chief Reyes enter. My mom seated him at one of my tables.

"Hello, Chief Reyes," I greeted him and gave him a menu.

"Hi, Cassie," he smiled and took the menu. "How are you?"

"I'm good. I met one of your new hires today." Talking to Chief Reyes could help verify Sean's job. Not that she didn't trust Sean, but the chief was right here.

"Oh yeah? You met Sean O'Reilly?" Chief Reyes handed the menu back without even looking at it.

"I did." Nodding, I took the menu. "I take it you want the dinner special and a glass of water?"

"Yes, please." Chief Reyes pointed to the booth opposite him. "Have a seat. Tell me what you think of Sean."

"Let me put your order in. I'll be right back." The front door jingled again, announcing a new patron. I watched Elias step inside and wait to be seated. My mom grabbed a menu and directed him to one of my open tables. Elias waved and smiled at me. I gave him a slight grin. Oh crap, now I had to serve him here.

"Cassie?" I felt Chief Reyes' hand on my elbow. "Are you okay? Do you know that guy?"

"Uh, yeah. He comes to the coffee shop every morning. It's all good." I smiled at Chief Reyes and pretended Elias' arrival didn't bother me.

Using my customer service fake smile, I walked to Elias' table.

"Hi Elias, are you ready to order?"

"Hi Cassie. I didn't know you worked here? It's nice to see you."

Maybe he wasn't who I saw sneaking around the parking lot earlier today when I was talking to Sean.

"Nice to see you, too." I lied. "What would you like to drink?"

"I'll have a water and a burger with fries, please."

"How would you like that cooked?"

"Rare." Eww, Cassie thought. I like my meat cooked all the way—no possibility of any mooing.

With his menu in hand, I swiftly placed his and the chief's food orders with my dad before I filled up two glasses of water.

"Do you know that man?" Mom whispered as she got some drinks for her customers.

"He comes to the coffee shop every morning."

"He asked to sit at your table, but he's giving me the creeps the way he keeps staring at you." Mom placed her hand on my arm. "He's making me nervous. Be careful around him."

"I will, but he's harmless. He watches me at the coffee shop, too. Just ignore him. He'll go away soon enough." I grabbed the drinks and dropped one off with Elias before I placed Chief Reyes' water in front of him and slid into the booth opposite him.

"So, what did you think?" Chief Reyes said after he took a drink.

"About what?" I had already forgotten our previous conversation. Out of the corner or my eye, I could see Elias staring at me.

"Sean O'Reilly. What did you think of him?"

"He seems very nice."

"That's it?" Chief Reyes stared at her.

"Uh, yeah." I reorganized the ketchup, mustard, and sugar packets in the table caddy.

"I heard you went with him to see a house." Chief Reyes raised his eyebrow.

"Sometimes, I hate small towns," I mumbled and sat deflated.

"No, you don't. You love it here."

"Chief Reyes." Sammie, one of my best friends who just moved back after several years of being away, stopped by our table with her triplets. Sammie moved away for a guy, but when she got pregnant with triplets, he only lasted a few months. After years of being a single mom, she moved back in with her mom and worked at her mother's boutique. "Stop questioning my favorite waitress and friend. Kids, go to that table. It's one of Cassie's. I'll be there in a minute."

"Hi, Sammie, kids," Chief Reyes smiled at her and waved to her kids. "I wasn't interrogating Cassie. She'll be there in just a second."

"See ya in a few." Sammie leaned down and gave me a quick side hug.

I didn't miss the look in Chief Reyes's eyes as he watched Sammie walk away. Did he like her? Interesting. It made sense because Cody the Chief's son was the same age as Sammie's triplets.

"I went with Sean to see widow Mary's house because he asked me. It's what any friend would do, right?" I shrugged.

"Whatever you say." Chief Reyes chuckled and glanced toward Elias. "Is there a reason that guy is staring at you?"

"He comes to the coffee shop a lot. He asked me out once and I said no." I shrugged.

Chief Reyes pointed to Sammie's table. "You might want to take their orders before Sammie has a mutiny on her hands. Those kids look hungry."

I glanced over and laughed. "They do, don't they? Where's Cody?" I was used to seeing Cody, Chief Reyes' son, with Holden, Sammie's male triplet.

"He's with my mom and dad. Grandma promised to bake him cookies, and he didn't want to pass that up."

"That's sweet." I slid out of the booth. "Tell him and your parents I said hello. Let me get their order, and then I'll check on your food."

"Sounds good, thanks." Chief Reyes nodded.

"Hey kids," I said when I got to Sammie's table. "What are you guys having?"

"Chicken Nuggets with Mac and Cheese," Hallie answered first.

"Same as Hallie." Hollie pointed to her sister.

"A burger with cheddar cheese and fries." Holden handed his menu to his mom.

"Can I get a fish dinner plate with double veggies instead of rice?" Sammie smiled at me.

"Of course." I wrote their orders. "What do you guys want to drink?"

The kids said soda, but Sammie shook her head and said directly to me. "Cassie, they will have water." After much grumbling from the kids, I walked away to put their order in and check on Elias and Chief Reyes' food.

I dropped off Elias' food first so I would have an excuse not to get stuck talking to him.

"Here you go, Chief." I placed his plate in front of him.

"Thanks, Cassie."

I walked away but noticed how the chief kept looking over at Sammie's table. I sat with Sammie and her kids for a few minutes.

"That guy staring at you gives me the creeps, Cassie." Sammie shivered.

"You and everyone else." I got up. "Let me get him his check so he can leave. I'll be back in a minute."

After I dropped off the check at Elias' table, a rush of customers came in and I didn't have time to check on him again. When it slowed back down, all I thought about was Sean and how much I missed him.

That thought scared me. My emotions were moving so fast, like a speeding train, that I couldn't seem to stop. How could I feel so strongly about Sean when I just met him a few hours ago? I'd never experienced love at first sight before, but that's how I felt. He made me so happy with all his compliments and kindness, yet it also terrified me.

Every one of my exes said sweet things to me until I told them I wasn't leaving Haven Island. I wanted to believe Sean, but only time would tell. This was the first time I told a potential boyfriend about my fears of being dumped. Fingers crossed, he would be the one to understand me and not hurt me like the others, but my parents were right. I had to open my heart up. If I kept it closed, I might never meet the love of my life. I had to give Sean a chance.

Sean: I miss you. How's work?

Cassie: Miss you, too. Work's good. I've gotten some good tips. Your toast worked.

Sean: I'm glad.

Cassie: Your new boss is here.

Sean: Chief Reyes?

Cassie: Yep.

Sean: Did you say nice things about me or throw me under the bus?

Cassie: Nice things, of course.

> Sean: Thank you. That's sweet of you. See you tomorrow at 11?

> Cassie: I'll be there. I'll meet you at the outdoor restaurant.

> Sean: I'll get us a table. Have a good night.

> Cassie: You too

The restaurant closed at eight; after a long shift, I walked out with my parents, the night air cool on my skin. Heading toward my car, I noticed a gray sedan parked in the back of the coffee shop. Strange.

"Whoever left their car there, I hope it's gone by the time you open tomorrow." Her dad sighed. "Don't they know better than to block the parking spots?"

"I'm sure they'll be gone in the morning." I hugged my dad. "If they're not, I'll call a tow truck."

"Okay, baby girl." Dad kissed my cheek and stepped back.

"Bye, honey." Mom hugged me. "We'll see you at home."

They waited until l got in my car, shut the door, and started the engine. As I pulled out of the parking lot, I saw the gray car peel out. Great, one less thing to worry about tomorrow. I waited for my parents to get behind me and they followed me home.

Chapter 9

# A Day with My Beautiful Girl

## Sean

By eleven on Sunday, I was bouncing off the walls. I couldn't wait to see Cassie again. Which was strange because I hadn't felt like that since I started dating Kerri. I put on some board shorts and a t-shirt and headed downstairs to the restaurant by the pool.

The first thing that hit me was the smell of fresh barbecue, thick with the scent of grilling meat and wood smoke. I saw smoke rising from the grill. It smelled delicious. Not only was there meat on the grill, but corn on the cob and grilled veggies. I found a table where I could sit facing the back of the hotel so I could see Cassie when she arrived and could wave her over.

A waitress came by and dropped off a menu. I asked for water, deciding to wait for Cassie before I ordered my meal and drink. Smiling, I watched several kids playing in the water. Their giggling was infectious.

"Are you waiting for someone?" the waitress asked after she placed my glass of water before me.

"Yes," I smiled. "She should be here soon."

"Okay, I'll be back."

I opened my messages app and double checked she was meeting me at 11:00am. Checking my watch, I realized she was a few minutes late. I hope she was okay. This island was not big enough to get lost, and she was a local.

I was getting ready to shoot her a text when I glanced up and saw her walking my way with a smile on her face. She was wearing a flowy white cover-up cinched at the waist and a big straw hat like a famous movie star. I couldn't wait to see her bathing suit and silently prayed that it was a bikini.

"Hi." Cassie set down her beach bag and sat. "Were you waiting long?"

"Nope, I just got here a few minutes ago."

"Have you ordered?" Cassie took off her hat and placed it on the seat next to her.

"I was waiting for you."

Cassie wasn't wearing any makeup. She was absolutely stunning.

"Hey Cassie." The waitress came back. "What would you like to drink?"

"Hi Darla. Can I just get some water for now?"

"Sure. I'll be back and take your order."

"What are you going to get?" Cassie asked while she stared at the menu.

I was having a hard time keeping my eyes off her. "What's good?"

Cassie leaned forward and covered the side of her mouth before she whispered, "every-thing. But don't tell my mom or dad I said so." Then she winked and sat back. "Honestly, this hotel is famous for their amazing barbecue brisket."

I liked this playful Cassidy. I mean, I liked the snarky one too, but this one was so at ease. "Then I think that's what I'll get." I closed my menu and placed it in front of me.

"Are you guys ready?" Darla had her pen and pad ready to write. "Ladies first."

"I'll have the barbecue chicken, corn on the cob, and a Piña Colada." Cassie handed her the menu.

I smirked because my girl loved her Piña Coladas and today it wasn't a virgin one.

"I'll have the barbecue brisket with grilled veggies and a Rum Runner."

"Sounds good." The waitress took our menus and left.

"Will you be able to spend the day with me?" I asked Cassie and took a sip of water.

"How long do you want to stay at the beach? With a last name of O'Reilly, I'm guessing you're Irish, and I'm not sure if you tan or burn."

"Oh, honey, I tan. My last name might be O'Reilly, but my mom was from Portugal, so I don't burn as easily as a full-blooded Irishman. But feel free to lather me up with suntan lotion in case the sun up here is stronger than the sun in South Florida." I wiggled my eyebrows at her.

"Is that one of your go to lines for the ladies?" Cassie rolled her eyes.

"Nope, that one is just for you." I sat back in my chair and stretched my legs. "But since you don't like it, how about at the end of the day, you show me your tan lines and I'll show you mine?"

Cassie busted out laughing. "Oh my God, they just get worse."

I shrugged. "Let's eat so we can get wet."

"Stop! Just stop." Cassie held her hand up and shook her head. "Those are horrible."

I loved hearing her laugh. It was music to my soul, and it warmed me throughout. Our food arrived, and the satisfying flavors of my meal burst into my mouth. Cassie was right. This was the best barbecue brisket I'd ever had. The delicious meal was punctuated by the happy shrieks and excited splashing of children in the sparkling blue pool, the sun reflecting brilliantly off the water's surface.

When we finished eating, we grabbed our stuff and found the umbrella and chairs that I'd reserved for the afternoon. Normally, I'd be strolling along the beach, feeling the sand between my toes and the gentle sea breeze on my face, or else stretched out on a towel, letting the warm sun bake my skin, but I wanted Cassie to be comfortable. I was telling Cassie the truth. I don't burn easily.

"Thank you for renting the beach chairs." Cassie sat down as I opened the umbrella. "Normally, I bring my own, but I totally forgot to put it in my car."

"No problem. Do you want to go for a walk?"

"I would love to after that lunch." Cassie smiled. "But let me put on my sunscreen."

Shit, I'd totally forgotten to buy some sunscreen. I don't burn, but I also wasn't stupid enough to put nothing on. "I'll be right back."

"Where are you going?"

"I need to buy some sunscreen in the gift shop."

"No need. I have 30 or 50 you can use." Cassie dug around in her purse and held them out to me. "Pick your poison."

"I'll take the 50 since I need to start my base tan because I'm so white." I cocked an eyebrow at her.

"You're not that pale." Cassie rolled her eyes and took off her flowy cover up.

Holy mother of God. Her body was like a wet dream in her leopard bikini. How the hell was I supposed to concentrate on anything when she looked like that? I should've been applying my sunscreen, but I felt frozen to my spot as I watched her run her hands over her legs, thighs, stomach, arms, and finally her chest.

"Why are you staring at me like that?" Cassie whispered.

"You are stunningly beautiful." I mumbled as I watched the pink blush rising from her perfect breasts to her smooth face.

"Can you put some sunscreen on my back?"

"It would be my pleasure."

I squeezed the lotion bottle, and the creamy liquid flowed onto my hands, releasing a coconut scent as I rubbed my hands together, warming it up before applying it to her skin. She put her hair in a ponytail, giving me total access to her slender back. With slow, deliberate strokes, I rubbed the lotion onto her shoulders. Feeling the warmth of her skin beneath my fingertips, I continued massaging her back long after the lotion absorbed because I didn't want to stop caressing her. I slipped my fingers under the back hook of her bathing suit and around the side, barely skimming the sides of her breasts.

Dreams of rubbing the lotion all over her naked body consumed me and I felt myself harden in my board shorts. Shit. I had to calm down. There were kids around us and I didn't need my bathing suit to tent out like a randy teen.

As soon as I finished applying her sunscreen, I cleared my throat, realizing I could no longer use that as a reason to touch her. "Will you do my back?"

"Of course." She stood and reached for the lotion.

I felt her small fingers rub the lotion onto my back with just the right amount of pressure. What I would give for a full body massage from her. After she finished my back, I quickly did my legs, arms, face, and chest.

"Let's walk." I grabbed her hand and led her to the packed sand.

Intertwining our hands together, we walked along the shore feeling the water splashing our ankles.

"Thank you for coming out to spend the day with me." I squeezed her hand.

"Thank you for inviting me." She squeezed back.

"What do you normally do on your day off?" I wanted to know everything about her. What she loved? What she hated? Her hobbies.

"I normally go to the park or come here and read. The ocean has a way of rejuvenating me and helping me decompress before the work week."

"I understand that."

"You're from South Florida. Did you live by the beach?"

"No. I lived further inland. I didn't get to the beach as often as I'd like, so it will be great to live closer. I'm like you." I pulled her closer to me. "The beach helps to center and calm me."

We continued walking for a few miles before we turned back and sat in our chairs.

I needed a drink. "Do you want something from the bar?"

"No, I'm good. I'm gonna lay on my stomach for a bit."

I watched Cassie lie on her stomach and undo her bikini straps. My board shorts instantly tented. The last thing I should have been doing was feeling the smooth, warm skin of her back, but the silken touch was too tempting to ignore, and I couldn't stop myself from asking. "Do you want me to reapply lotion on your back?"

"That would be great." Cassie pointed to her bag. "Use the 30."

I reached for the bag and kneeled beside her, not giving a fuck that my knees were sinking into the sand. Zeroing in on her back, I squirted lotion on my hands and massaged her shoulders again. Between the softness of her skin and the smell of the suntan lotion, I was about to explode in my board shorts like a teenage boy.

Gliding my hands over her lower back, I slid my hands up her sides and brushed the sides of her breasts. My breaths were coming in harsher and I heard her give a low moan. Oh, how I wished this was a secluded beach, and we were the only ones here.

# Beach Time Vibes

## Cassie

The massage felt absolutely glorious. His hands were just the right amount of pressure to relax my muscles and turn me on. I loved a good massage as foreplay. When his fingers reached closer to my breasts and I felt the gentle touch on the sides, it was like an electric current zipped down from my breasts to my core.

I know he heard my moan because I heard him take a harsh breath. I clenched my thighs, hoping he didn't notice. His hands traveled to my lower back and his fingers wrapped around my hips before he slowly slid the tips under my bikini bottom.

Sean was turning me into mush. My brain totally focused on the weight of his hands on my skin, the electric tingle of his touch, and the waves of heat he sent through me. The children's laughter, once bright and clear, faded into a distant echo, swallowed by the feelings he was awakening in my body. His hands left my body, only to return a few minutes later as they settled on my thighs. A shiver ran down my spine. His hands briefly slid under my bikini and cupped my ass. I never knew someone touching my ass could feel so warm and comforting.

Sliding his hands down, his fingers glided over the back of my thighs, a feather-light touch, sending shivers up my spine as they brushed against the delicate fabric of my bikini bottom at the junction of my thighs. Oh my goodness, he was a master with those hands. Before I could capture his hands between my legs, he applied suntan lotion to my calves and massaged the muscle.

That massage would feel so much better if I were facing him and he could run his hands over my body, cupping my breasts and playing with my nipples. I moaned again, and I was positive he heard me, if his chuckle was any sign.

"Your body is fully lotioned. I would be shocked if you burned anywhere because I didn't leave any patch of skin untouched."

I turned my head and saw him clean off his knees before he sat in his chair. The tent in his pants let me know how much his massage affected him. Maybe later we could redo the massage naked in his room.

"Thank you," I murmured.

Sean's heated gaze, eyes blazing with barely contained sexual frustration, betrayed his inner struggle for calmness.

"What are you smirking about?" He cocked an eyebrow at me.

"Just thinking how great your massages are, and I was hoping you might give me another one after we shower when we're alone in your room."

Sean leaned his head back and shut his eyes. "Fuck, are you trying to kill me?"

His chest was rising and falling at a surprisingly alarming rate. He reached his hand up to place them over his eyes, but I reached over and grabbed his hand.

"No! Don't touch your eyes. You have sunscreen on them."

Sean immediately opened his eyes and turned his head. His eyes bulging before he looked around. "You really are trying to kill me," he grunted before he threw his towel over my back. "For fuck's sake, woman, you just had your beautiful breasts on display. This is a family beach."

I had been so worried about protecting his eyes; I forgot my top was undone. I felt a breeze over my nipples right before his towel draped over me. Glancing around, I realized no one was paying attention except for Elias, who was staring at me and licking his lips. Eww.

"I'm so embarrassed." I cowered under his towel.

"I don't think anyone saw anything."

"Except for creepy Elias behind us to my right."

"I don't see who you're talking about."

I reached back and tied my bikini before I leaned up. Elias was gone. Was it my imagination? Maybe he had been looking for someone. "He's not there."

"How about we go in the water? I need to cool down." Sean stood and put his hand out to help me.

"I could use a cool down, too."

Sean helped me up, and we walked into the ocean. The water felt refreshing against my heated skin. Sean was much taller than me, but he stopped when the water reached my waist. Bending down, he submerged his entire body.

"This feels good, but why are you so far away from me?" Sean gave me what looked like his smouldering look.

"I thought you wanted to cool down?"

"I do, but come here." Sean grabbed my hand and pulled my body into his. Between his strength and the current, I sat on his lap, facing him. I wrapped my legs around his waist. "This is much better." Sean smiled and rubbed my back. "Let's play a game. Two truths and a lie."

I chuckled, "Okay."

"My best friend's girlfriend was roofied. I caught my ex-girlfriend in our bedroom being intimate with another woman. And I used to drive a minivan."

"Oh, my God." I covered my mouth with my hand. "Was your best friend's girlfriend okay?"

"She was. We got to her in time. So, which one of the other two do you think is the lie?"

"You don't look like the minivan type." I tapped my finger on my lips. "Then again, who would cheat on you with someone else, let alone another woman?"

I wasn't sure which one to go with, so I went with the most obscure one. "You caught your girlfriend with another girl."

"Okay, so it's a half truth. I caught her cheating on me, but it was with another guy."

I winced. "Ouch."

"Yep, after I caught them, I kicked her out and left town for a change of scenery."

My mouth hung open. "You drove a minivan?"

"Yep, for about six months. My ex wanted me to show her I was ready for commitment and a family."

"Maybe she should've driven the minivan." Cassie mumbled wryly.

We both got a laugh out of my comment.

"Okay, your turn." Sean nodded at me.

"I have a tattoo of a butterfly on my hip. I played volleyball in high school. And I burn myself at least once a day with the coffee pot at work."

"I would love to see your tattoo." Sean rubbed his thumbs over my hips.

I made a sound like a buzzer. "Wrong. No tattoo."

"You can't be over five foot three. How the hell did you play volleyball in high school?"

"It was beach volleyball, and I was good at diving for the ball."

"Baby, you could dive for my balls anytime." Sean wiggled his eyebrows.

"Eeww." I smacked his shoulders and pushed off. "I can't believe you just said that." I acted as though offended, but in truth, I would love to dive for any part of his body. The water was supposed to calm me down, but the entire time I sat on his lap, I could feel him hardening.

We splashed around in the water for a few more minutes before we went back to our beach chairs. This time I sat on my ass and didn't undo my top. I didn't see Elias anywhere. I must've imagined him. As the sun set, we gathered up our stuff and headed back to his room. We agreed to get cleaned up and go to dinner.

# Chapter 11

# Welcome to Haven Island PD

## Sean

Spending the day with Cassie yesterday had been fantastic. She was so easy to talk to about anything. I wanted to see her this morning, so I drove to the coffee shop where she worked. Not having received my police uniform yet, I was in a suit and tie.

I left the hotel well before my meeting with Chief Reyes, so I could go into 'Hi Café' and watch her while I drank my first cup of coffee for the day. Parking was easy since most people were pulling through the drive-thru. The inside was busy with customers ordering or enjoying their morning java.

Cassie worked the register, while a younger, similarly dark-haired girl handled the drive-thru. I stood in line and waited my turn. Cassie took orders, then crafted each coffee with precision. Topping each cup off with her genuine smile as she called the customer's names.

When it was my turn, Cassie graced me with her brightest smile like a ray of sunshine. A smile that I would love to see at the start of every day for the rest of my life. Wow, I was falling for her pretty damn fast. How could I not? She was smart, beautiful, funny, and kind.

"Good morning. What can I get you?"

"Good morning, sunshine." I winked at her. This was the best way to start my first day on the job. "Can I get a cup of black coffee?"

"That's it?" Cassie scrunched up her nose. "You don't want to try our latte, mocha, or cappuccino?"

"I usually just drink it black," I smirked at her and she rolled her eyes. "Okay for you and since it's my first day at work, give me a cappuccino and a blueberry muffin."

Her eyes bulged out of her head, and her mouth dropped open.

I chuckled. "Why are you looking at me like that?" What had I said that shocked her silent?

"You are going to eat carbs? What will the protein and veggie police say? Are you supposed to run miles today on your first day?"

"Okay, smartass," I grinned at her. "I'm not sure when I'll have time to eat lunch and I wanted something that might fill me up. But you're right, I need some protein, so throw in something that has an egg in it, would you?"

"As you wish." Cassie bowed and rang up my order.

I paid and took my receipt. As I put my wallet in my back pocket, I noticed her stiffen before she said hello to the customer behind me. Was she okay? Did she know him? Did he usually bother her?

I found an empty table and watched their interaction, the clatter of dishes and murmur of conversation filling the air, waiting to see if Cassie needed my help, but the guy just placed his order and sat at an open table. Leaning back in my chair, I observed everyone in the café. When my order was ready, Cassie called my name, and I went to get it.

I wanted to ask her to sit with me for a few minutes, but with only two of them there, she wasn't gonna be able to have a cup of coffee with me. Several officers and firefighters came in and joked with her. I noticed none of them had to give her their order. She knew exactly what they wanted and handed it to them as soon as it was ready. I never saw her charge them, but they all put money in her tip jar–and we're talking larger bills.

After I finished my coffee and meal, I stood and waited until she made eye contact. I waved and made the universal sign for call me. She smiled, and I left. I didn't want to be late on my first day because of my infatuation with my girl.

The island wasn't big, and it took me no time to get to the station. The officer at the front desk greeted me at the door.

"How can I help you, sir?"

"I have a meeting with Chief Reyes."

"Your name?"

"Sean O'Reilly."

"Welcome Officer O'Reilly." The officer stood and shook my hand. "I'm Officer Jenkins. We are so glad to have you."

"Thank you."

"Follow that hallway," the officer pointed with his thumb over his shoulder, "and the Chief's office is the first door on your right."

"Got it. Thanks again." I nodded and followed the hallway to the glass door with the nameplate that read Chief Alejandro Reyes.

Chief Reyes was a tall, muscular man of Spanish descent, with gray sprinkled throughout his beard and hair. When I knocked on the slightly ajar door, he immediately looked up, smiled, and waved me in before he stood with his hand outstretched.

"Hello, Sean. Welcome to Haven Island PD."

"Hi Chief Reyes." I shook his hand. "It's nice to meet you in person."

"Have a seat. I heard you put an offer in on widow Mary's house." Chief sat and shuffled some papers into a folder on his desk.

"I guess I'm gonna have to get used to everyone knowing my business, huh?"

"Yep. This island is like a small town. The locals are always gossiping and the tourists are oblivious. I hope you like it here, coming from the city."

"I'm sure I will. Sunrise was a sleepy town when I first moved there too. I'm looking forward to going back to that."

"I have some paperwork for you to fill out." Chief Reyes placed a folder in front of him. "But first, let's go into our squad room so you can meet everyone. We usually meet every Monday morning. When we're done, you can come back to my office to fill out all the forms, then I'll give you a tour and you can get your uniforms. I hope you don't mind patrolling with a partner this afternoon? Hudson can give you a lay of the land."

We entered the squad room—a rectangular space furnished with three rows of six-foot tables and chairs. A podium and whiteboard stood at the front of the room.

"I brought coffee from Hi Café, if you want a cup." Chief Reyes pointed to the table on the side of the room with a huge to-go container of coffee, cups, creamers, and sugars. "When you finish, come to the podium so I can introduce you."

"Sounds good, thanks."

I'd already had a cup of coffee, but decided on another. Some men were already filing in and heading for the coffee. I could hear their conversations, but didn't want to butt in.

"So, you're the new guy, huh?" A man in a suit who reminded me of George glanced my way as he filled his cup. "I'm Detective Lucian Warrick."

"Hi." I shook his hand. "I'm Sean O'Reilly. Good to meet you."

"It's nice to meet you too."

The detective was about to say something when an officer standing behind me spoke up. "Detective, you will be here in your cushy job all day. Don't hog all the coffee."

Several officers laughed. I wasn't sure how to take it. Would the detective enjoy the sarcastic banter, or would he get pissed? He didn't have to wait long before he saw a smile on the detective's face.

"Well, Hudson, if you worked harder maybe you could get a detective job instead of being a beat cop for the rest of your sorry ass life."

"Oh, snap," another officer guffawed.

"Yeah, yeah, yeah." Hudson reached behind me and lightly punched the detective's shoulder. "I'll get there one day even though I'm not a Warrick."

As soon as Detective Warrick finished making his coffee, he walked to Hudson and put the hand not holding his cup on his shoulder. "I'm sure you will. You're a good cop."

"Thanks, man," Hudson smiled. "I appreciate that."

Sean poured his cup of black coffee and strolled to the front of the room next to Chief Reyes.

"I see you already met Lucian." Chief Reyes leaned against the podium, waiting for everyone to get their coffee.

"I did." I nodded. "He seems cool."

I stood with Chief Reyes until everyone grabbed their coffee and settled down. I loved seeing their camaraderie. It was something I enjoyed when I worked in South Florida and hoped to have in this new job.

"Okay, settle down. I'll make it brief. We have a new officer starting today." Chief Reyes turned to face me. "This is Sean O'Reilly. He just moved here from Sunrise, where he was a patrol officer and field training officer for the Sunrise Sheriff's Department. He will ride along with Hudson this afternoon. Tuesday, he'll go with Sawyer, Wednesday with Roman, Thursday with Ryker and K9 Judge, and Friday with Charlotte. I want him to get a lay of the land before we set him loose next week. Let's give him a warm welcome."

Everyone clapped or waved. I did a quick wave and took my coffee with me to an empty seat in the middle of the first row. Yep, just like back home, no one liked to sit in the front row and if they did, it was the seats at the end by the door for a quick exit. After I sat, Detective Lucian slapped my back and said, "Welcome aboard."

I nodded, set my cup down, and waited for Chief Reyes to continue. He went over several jobs that were still outstanding and summarized finished jobs.

"Unless there are any impeding issues, I'll see you all back here next Monday for our usual squad room meeting. Until then, stay safe out there, boys." Chief Reyes gathered all his papers and shoved them into a folder. "On your way out, please introduce yourselves to Sean—especially those who'll be riding with him this week. Make sure he knows who you are."

"Thanks, Chief," most of them hollered back.

"Sean," Hudson screamed out from behind him. "You ready to roll, man?"

"I have some paperwork to fill out."

Chief Reyes came up behind them. "Why don't you take it home and go with Hudson? It'll be fine if you turn it in tomorrow."

"Thank you, sir." I nodded.

## Chapter 12

# A Temporary Partner

## Sean

"**I**'m ready whenever you are." I smiled at Hudson.

Several officers took the time to introduce themselves on our way out. The impression was one of a friendly brotherhood, despite my inability to remember all their names; a strong sense of mutual respect and easy companionship. I kept hearing the last name Warrick. I've had the pleasure of working with many sibling pairs and father-son teams in my past positions. In many families, it's a calling, passed down through generations, a legacy of service and dedication.

Before I joined, my father spent years as a beat cop in South Florida, patrolling sun-baked streets, while dealing with some truly unhinged individuals. The dangers of being a cop were clear to me as I saw my father put on his uniform and holster his gun before he left for work. I watched my father struggle with the ever-present risk of injury, the emotional toll of witnessing trauma, and the gut-wrenching potential for loss of life; however, it didn't deter me from joining the force. I inherited a legacy of service, just like my father and grandfather; it ran through my veins like a second heartbeat. When Kerri voiced her concern over my dangerous job, the sincerity in her voice was clear, but I had to explain to her that being a law enforcement officer was my lifelong dream.

I knew the dangers of being a cop. Hell, I lived it. But being an officer was in my blood, like my father and grandfather. When Kerri voiced her opinion about me getting hurt, I was well aware of her concern, but I had to make her understand that my lifelong dream had always been to become a police officer. My deep-seated need to protect and serve was why I'd formed such a strong bond with my previous partner, George. The same relentless energy to assist those in need, the same inner fire that burned within me, shone brightly in George. I already missed the everyday companionship I had with George, but was glad to have found another accepting brotherhood.

I followed Hudson to his patrol vehicle and got in on the passenger side. Looking around the inside, I realized it looked just like the cars we drove in Sunrise.

"Does it look like yours from down south?" Hudson started it up and pulled out of the parking lot.

"Yep. I guess once you've seen one, you've seen them all."

"The state probably gets them from the same place. We used to drive sedans, but finally upgraded to these small SUV's with the pursuit package and four-wheel drive. I can't tell you how many times we've had to drive on the sand. Usually it's getting to a tourist who's in trouble, but we've had to haul cars and catch suspects who run toward the water."

"Do they not realize unless they have a boat, it's a long swim to the mainland?" I stared at him with my mouth open.

"I guess once they get to the shore, they feel committed. Sawyer usually gets those calls. He's our dive team expert. He also has a small boat, so he can get to them if they are already too far out."

"Wow, so several of you do double duty?"

"Yep, we're a small unit. When we need backup, we call the mainland and they send some of their deputies to assist. You met all the guys at the meeting. I'm also on the SWAT team and the Dive Team, although mostly I patrol. We're fortunate to not require a full SWAT team, which is a good thing."

"I'm glad." Glancing at his computer, I saw the calls coming in. "I wanted to move to a smaller town and leave the craziness of the city behind. Not that I want nothing to do. I love working, but Sunrise was getting crazy with the gangs, motorcycle clubs, and human trafficking."

"The most we see around here are drug busts, tourists that get too drunk, speeding, and sometimes we find someone hiding from the mainland cops, and we have to serve a warrant. You'll be busy. This isn't Mayberry, but it won't be like the city."

"I can live with that. I'd like to do double duty too whenever it's offered." I looked out the window, orienting myself with the city streets.

"Talk to the chief. He loves go-getters." Hudson grinned.

We drove around the island. Hudson pointed out places I needed to know about. I told him about the closing of my house on Wednesday and around lunchtime; we stopped at Hi Grill for lunch.

"I love this place." Hudson said before he stepped out of the car. "They have the best burgers in town and the girls are easy on the eyes."

I wondered if he was talking about Cassie or her sister. Had he dated Cassie? As soon as they entered, Cassie's mom came over with menus to seat them.

"Hello officers," Judy smiled. "Just two for lunch?"

"Yes, ma'am," Hudson smiled.

"Follow me."

Cassie's mom led us to a booth by the front windows. I looked around and saw Cassie walk out of the kitchen carrying several plates. With her radiant smile and flowing dress, she was truly a sight to behold. I was in awe of her and wondered how she did it. Working early in the morning at the coffee shop and then here until eight.

"Cassie will be right with you," Judy said before she walked away.

I looked over the menu and ordered the burger since Hudson gave it such rave reviews. Besides, I could always go for a run along the beach or work out in the hotel gym tonight.

"Hello Hudson, Sean," Cassie said respectively when she approached our table. "What are you having today?"

"Hey, beautiful." Hudson winked at her. "I'll have the burger all the way with fries and a coke."

Shit. Hudson liked Cassie. This was going to get ugly. But wait, Cassie told me the officers often flirted with her when they went to the coffee shop. She swore it was all in good fun.

"Hey, Cass." I gave her my best smile. "I'll have the same, but with water."

"Wow, no fish today?" Cassie cocked her eyebrow at me.

"Nope, Hudson said you have the best burgers, and I wanted to give them a shot." I shrugged and handed her the menu.

"Well, okay then." Cassie took my menu and Hudsons before she left our table.

"Cass?" Hudson grinned. "Do you know Cassie?"

"We just met on Saturday when I came into town. I came here to eat, and we got to talking." I wasn't sure if I should tell him she went house shopping with me and we spent the day at the beach.

"Cool. Cassie is great. I've asked her sister out several times, but she's so fucking busy, we haven't been able to set a date. Maybe you can be my wingman?"

"I'll try as long as it's her sister you want and not Cass."

"I heard my name." Cassie set the glasses of water on the table and stared at me. "Did you need something?"

"Uh, no. I was just telling Hudson that we've already met and are friends."

"Yep." Cassie nodded at Hudson. "I put your orders in. I'll bring them as soon as they're ready."

"Thanks," they both muttered.

"So, how long have you lived here?" I took a sip of my water. Damn, that cool water tasted good. I'll have to fill up a water bottle tomorrow and bring it with me while out on patrol. I always had one back home, not sure why I didn't bring one today.

"I grew up here. Never wanted to go anywhere else."

"I can see why. It's beautiful here."

Cassie came back and delivered our food. I took a healthy bite of my burger and decided it was the best burger I'd ever eaten. After I finished chewing, I ate a fry washing it down with some water.

"This is the best burger ever. I'm glad you suggested it. Do you guys ever work nights?"

"We do." Hudson swallowed. "We rotate after ninety days. Is that how you did it down south?"

"Yep." Great, I was used to that drill.

After lunch, I continued to stare out the window, watching the scenery and local businesses we were driving by as Hudson pointed them out and gave a bit of history behind them. We had a traffic stop and a drunk tourist, but other than that, it was a quiet afternoon.

## Chapter 13

# House Closing

## Cassie

Today was Sean's closing. I couldn't wait to hear how it went. If I wasn't so swamped with customers, I'd shoot him a quick text wishing him luck, but the line never seemed to get any shorter. Ready for my next customer, I looked up.

"Good morning." I smiled and saw Elias. "What can I get you? The usual?"

Elias always ordered a large, hot Mocha Latte. When he nodded, I turned around and made it. Having worked as a barista throughout high school and college, making coffee was second nature; but with Elias watching, I worked even faster. Setting the coffee down in front of him, I rang up his order.

"That'll be $6.41."

"Do you want to get dinner tonight?" Elias asked through gritted teeth.

I certainly wasn't going out with him, but seeing his anger, I tried to let him down as kindly as possible.

"I'm sorry. I can't." I gave him one of my fake smiles. The ones that never reach my eyes. "I have plans with a friend."

"A guy friend?" Elias squeezed his cup of coffee so hard, the lid popped off and some coffee spilled on the counter.

I knew the coffee was hot, but he never even flinched.

"Hey, man. Are you okay?" Officer Hudson asked Elias.

Elias released the cup and wiped his hand on his pants before he grabbed the cup again and glared at me.

"Cassie, are you okay?" Officer Charlotte stepped up beside Elias and grabbed some napkins to clean the coffee that spilled on the other side of the counter.

"I'm fine." I grabbed a few napkins and wiped my side of the counter while Elias stood staring at me. "Is there anything else you need, Elias?"

"No," he grunted, slapped a ten-dollar bill on the counter, and stormed out.

Watching Elias leave, Charlotte turned to me and asked, "Is that guy giving you trouble?"

"No, it's fine." I shook my head and smiled. "He's harmless. He wanted a date, and I said no."

"Okay, but if he comes back and gets ornery again, call us." Charlotte squeezed my hand before releasing it.

"I will. Thanks." I nodded. "Now, what can I get you guys?"

I hadn't seen Elias again after the morning incident. When my coffee shop shift ended, I drove to the restaurant because it was my day to work there until closing. To give my sister and me more time off during the summer, our parents hired an extra waitress. Today was her first day, and it was my turn to train the new employee.

I received a text message from Sean around five.

> **Sean:** Closing is over. I just bought a house. Come over.

> **Cassie:** I'm still at work. Training a new waitress.

> **Sean:** Until?

> **Cassie:** Around 8 maybe.

> **Sean:** OK. Come by after. They left a grill. I'll make dinner.

> **Cassie:** OK. I'll bring dessert

> **Sean:** You are dessert

Oh, my word. Every time I saw or talked to that man, he made me feel flustered and excited, even through text messages. I fanned my face, trying to cool down from the heat emanating from his text.

"Are you okay, honey?" My mom walked by me with plates.

"Oh, yeah. I'm good. Just hot."

"I can ask your father to turn down the air conditioner."

"No, no. I'm good."

I looked at my phone when I heard the beep of another incoming message.

Sean: Sorry, was that too much?

Cassie: No, it's just busy. I'll see you around 8.

Sean: Okay.

I finished my shift, on pure muscle memory. I couldn't remember who came in or what they ordered. All I could think about was how exciting it would be to see Sean; my heart pounded with anticipation. No one had ever referred to me as dessert.

Chapter 14

# New House, New Chapter

## Sean

I ran to the grocery store and bought some chicken and veggies to put on the grill, salad, and a bottle of wine to toast my new house. I knew Cassie would give me shit for a healthy dinner choice, but I was sure her choice of dessert would be enough calories. My girl liked her sweets.

I marinated the chicken in a spicy blend of herbs and chilies, then chopped the vibrant vegetables before wrapping them up in two aluminum foil packets; the aroma filled the fridge until Cassie's arrival. I grabbed a glass of chilled white wine and settled into a wicker chair on my new back porch, enjoying the gentle breeze. Widow Mary left most of the furniture, including the outdoor patio set. She said she was moving into a room in her daughter's house and didn't have any space for it. I told her not to worry. Whatever I didn't want, I would donate. I eventually planned to buy my own furniture, but after Kerri took most of ours when she left, claiming she'd chosen it all, I was thankful for what Widow Mary left behind. I called bullshit, but let Kerri have the furniture. The last thing I wanted was to have another conversation with her.

The moving truck was bringing a spare bedroom set and a couch with my recliner. Kerri never liked my recliner. She said it was an eyesore in our house. Better for me since I loved it and got to keep it.

It was getting dark. I checked my watch and saw it was 7:45pm. I could start grilling, but what if Cassie had to stay later? It was better that I cook once she got here, so it would all be fresh and hot, right off the grill. Besides, chicken and veggies didn't take long to cook. I arranged the silverware, plates, and napkins neatly on the table, left the sliding glass door partially open so I could hear the doorbell, then sat back down in my chair. I stared at the frothy whitecaps of the waves rolling in, feeling the cool breeze on my face.

Twenty minutes later, I heard the doorbell. I had been looking forward to seeing her all day. With a burst of excitement, I threw open the door, a wide smile spreading across my face. She took my breath away as she stood there, beaming, in her floral summer dress falling to her thighs, a pastry box in her hands.

"Hey, welcome to my new home." I spread my arms wide.

"Hi." Cassie smiled and brought a pastry box to me. "I hope you like apple pie."

"I love apple pie. Did you make it?"

"You're funny." She snorted. "Mom made it."

"Do you cook?" I asked. Not really caring if she cooked or not, just curious.

"I can, but I don't seem to have a lot of time." Cassie placed it on the kitchen island.

"What's your favorite thing to cook?" I headed to the fridge and grabbed the Pinot Grigio I'd started earlier. After pouring her a glass, I put the wine back and took out the chicken and veggies.

"I don't have a favorite, but I do like baking cookies at Christmas."

"Well, you don't have to wait until Christmas. I love cookies." I winked at her. "You can bake me cookies anytime."

"I'll remember that. What can I do to help?"

Opening a drawer, I grabbed some tongs, and I waved her over. "Grab your glass and follow me. You can come keep me company while I grill."

Cassie followed me outside and sat on one of the deck chairs.

"Are you okay with us eating outside?" I asked as I placed the food on the grill.

"Absolutely." Cassie sat. "The ocean looks so peaceful tonight."

"It sure does." I closed the grill top and walked to her.

I slowly bent down, and with one finger, brushed her hair behind her ear and kissed her cheek. "I'm glad you came over."

Cassie smiled and took a sip of her wine. "I'm glad you invited me."

I took a sip of mine and stood beside her. "You are the only person I'd want to celebrate with tonight. I've missed you. I haven't seen you since Sunday. That's three whole days without seeing your beautiful face."

"Yeah, right?" Cassie smirked.

"I mean it, Cass." My voice got lower, and I slowly lowered my lips to hers, giving her a light kiss.

Cassie opened her mouth, but I didn't want to rush it tonight. I wanted to go slow and drive her as crazy as she drove me. With a slight kiss to her bottom lip, Cassie sighed, but I turned around to check on the chicken. Out of the corner of my eye, I saw her cross her legs and sip more wine.

I wanted her so desperately, but I also wanted to savor our moment together.

"You were so lucky to get this house. Most oceanfront properties are hard to find."

"I guess I was looking at the right time." The veggies were done and the chicken only had a couple more minutes left. "Can you go to the refrigerator and get the salad and dressing? I'm almost done here."

"Sure."

I waited until Cassie set the salad on the table, then said, "Bring me your plate and I'll put your chicken and veggies on it."

Cassie stood next to me, holding both our plates. I put the smaller aluminum foiled veggies packet and a chicken breast on hers and two chicken breasts and the larger aluminum packet on mine.

"What's in the aluminum foil?"

"Broccoli, zucchini, and squash." I answered her before I turned off the grill and closed the lid.

"Yummy." Cassie set my plate down and then hers. She opened her foil packet and steam puffed out. "This looks and smells fantastic. Thank you for making us dinner."

"You're welcome. It was my pleasure." I sat down and lifted my glass for a toast. "To my new home and my new friend. Thank you for your help in picking out this house." Cassie clinked her glass with mine.

I carefully dumped the veggies from the foil to my plate. "Let me remove that foil for you." Not wanting Cassie to burn herself, I grabbed her foil and mine and put them on the original tray I used to bring out the food.

Perfect. Now we could eat. "How was your day?"

"It started out crappy, but got better." Cassie cut up her chicken.

"Why was it crappy? When I left the coffee shop this morning, you were happy."

"Elias, one of my regulars, asked me out and when I said no, he got angry and spilled his coffee on the counter. It startled me. Luckily, some of your fellow officers were there, and he left."

"Was that the guy that you thought was at the beach? Has he given you trouble before?" I studied her expression closely, searching for any traces of nervousness.

"Not really. I mean, he's kind of creepy the way he looks at me, but he's never done anything." Cassie shrugged.

"What do you mean by the way he looks at you?" I was now on alert. I'd dealt with too many creepy men stalking my female friends in South Florida to last me a lifetime.

"Can we talk about something else?" Cassie wouldn't look at me. She kept eating her food like I wasn't there.

"Cass." I reached out and held her hand. "Is this guy stalking you?"

"No." Cassie squinted and stared out at the ocean. She looked lost in thought.

"Then why are you not looking at me? What are you thinking in that pretty little head of yours?"

"I thought I saw him the day I met you at the diner lurking behind a van, but when I looked again, no one was there. Then that day at the beach when I accidentally flashed my boobs, he was looking at my breasts, then he licked his lips before he looked down at his phone and walked away."

"Cass." I stood and pulled her into my arms. "You need to report this."

"I'm sure I could take him. He's pretty scrawny." Cassie chuckled.

"Don't make light of this, Cass. It's not funny. He doesn't need to be an enormous man to overtake you with the element of surprise. Please, promise me you'll be careful and you won't go anywhere alone at night."

"Sean, it'll be fine. Nothing like that happens here." Cassie shook her head.

"There's a first time for everything." I wrapped my arms around her. "I care about you. I don't want anything to happen to you."

"I care about you too," Cassie said breathlessly. "It's gonna be okay."

I couldn't help myself. I needed to taste her delicious lips again. Bending down, I ran my tongue along her bottom lip until she opened up for me. My tongue entered her mouth, and it felt like coming home. Her warmth and urgency to draw me closer to her was overwhelming. I'd never felt this crazy for a woman before. Cassie moaned, and I knew we needed to stop so I could feed her.

Slowly releasing her, I took a deep breath and waited until she opened her eyes and looked at me.

"We'll continue this later. For now, let's finish our meal. We still have dessert."

Her cheeks flushed. She must be remembering my comment about her being my dessert. It wasn't just a comment. It was a promise. I knew she would taste great with that apple pie slathered all over her body.

We finished eating in silence, both of us deep in our own thoughts. We shared several heated glances, but I refused to give in until she had a full stomach. I had a lot planned for tonight. She needed her strength.

## Chapter 15

# I Think I Love Him

## Cassie

As soon as we finished dinner, I stood and grabbed my plate.

"I got it." Sean snagged it out of my hands and stacked it on top of his. "You relax and enjoy the ocean."

"Thank you."

This was a pleasant change. Usually, I was the one serving and cleaning up dishes. I slipped off my shoes and leaned back in the chair. Closing my eyes, I propped my feet on the opposite chair. It was nice to smell the salty water and feel the ocean breeze at the end of a workday.

"Hey." Sean was crouched in front of me. "You tired?" He ran his hand down my cheek and brushed my hair behind my ears.

"It's been a long day." I smiled and sighed.

Sean sat in the chair across from me, pulled my feet onto his lap, and massaged the balls of my feet.

"Are you going to be staying here now? Did you check out of the hotel?"

"I did. Why spend money when I have this magnificent house with a beautiful view?"

"Mmm, that feels wonderful." I moaned.

"Keep moaning like that, and I'll have to take you inside." Sean looked around. "The neighbors might talk."

"Then let's take it inside." I slipped my feet off his lap and strolled to the sliding glass door. Turning to look over my shoulder, I winked. "Are you coming?"

"Yes, ma'am."

Sean grabbed our glasses and followed me inside. I recalled the location of the master bedroom and headed there. The need to be with him was overwhelming. He had awoken a spark in me I hadn't felt in a long time. The way he looked at me, like he wanted to devour me. No man had ever looked at me like that and still listened to the words coming out of my mouth.

Upon entering the room, I realized my mistake. There was no bed.

"So much for my seductive moves." I spun around. "You don't have a bed."

"We don't need a bed." Sean smiled sexily.

Placing our glasses on the cold, tiled floor with a soft clink, he shuffled toward me. His arms encircled me as he guided me backward toward the wall. "I just need you."

Sean gazed into my eyes and slowly lowered his mouth to mine. He licked my lips and gave a gentle bite until I opened my mouth. His tongue thrust into my mouth as my back hit the wall. Oh my goodness, this man's kisses were all-consuming. Grabbing my hands, he raised them above my head and held them there while he continued to ravish my mouth with his skillful tongue.

My head was swimming with desire. I needed him to use that tongue all over my body. I hadn't been with anyone in almost a year, and I was shaking with need. As if he read my mind, his left hand held me still while his right traveled down my arm, skimming the sides of my breasts before cupping them.

I let out a moan as he tweaked my nipple through my bra. A searing electric current surged through my entire body. I pushed my hips against his and he trapped them against the wall. Thrusting his hips in the same motion as his tongue.

He let go of my mouth and groaned while planting gentle kisses along my jawline and neck, pausing to suck firmly where my neck meets my shoulders. That was my sweet spot. As his mouth went around my neck to the opposite area, his hands traveled down to my bottom and gripped my ass, pulling me into him.

I was burning up inside. All I could think about was how he would feel inside me. I lowered my hands and ran them down his sculpted chest, leaving one at his side while the other continued to his shaft. I gripped him through his pants and heard him moan into my neck before he lifted his face to mine.

"Are you sure about this?" Sean gazed into my eyes.

"Yes."

"Come with me." Sean held his hand out and I placed my palm in his.

He was leading me out of the room and into another one.

"Widow Mary left the twin beds in this room."

Sean stopped and turned to me. Cupping my face, he gave me another one of his sensual kisses, taking my breath away. "I don't want to make love to you on the floor."

His choice of words made me feel special. He said make love, not fuck, that was promising. Maybe Sean wouldn't be another love 'em and leave 'em man. Sean sat on the edge of the bed and pulled me onto his lap. My legs on either side of his thighs.

"You can still back out at any time." Sean stared at me while he pulled his wallet out of his back pocket and pulled out a condom, laying it on the bed.

"I see you are prepared." I grinned.

"Not prepared, hopeful. I only have one. I would have an entire box if I had been prepared." Sean teased, cupped my face, and kissed me.

In a quick motion, he turned his body and laid me down flat on the bed. Dropping to his knees, he pulled me to the edge. Lightly running his hands up my legs as he skimmed my shins and inner thighs. When he reached my aching core, he moved his hands up to my hips. My dress was now hiked up to my waist.

He leaned forward and pressed his lips to my core through my lace panties.

"Although I love your panties, they need to go."

I couldn't even think of what to say to him. All I could do was feel the need he was awakening in my body. The need to wrap myself around him and feel him deep inside me. Sean pulled my panties off and dove into my core. His tongue thrusting inside while one hand played with my nub while the other held me in place. A staggering need for this man consumed my mind and body, leaving me breathless and wanting. I could feel my orgasm building with every stroke of his tongue and fingers, which alternated between licking, sucking, and thrusting at my core. Gripping the sheets, I climaxed harder than ever before. I saw bursts of lights behind my eyelids like fireworks. My screams were so loud I hoped the windows were closed.

As I took deep breaths, I felt the bed dip. Sean pulled me up to the headboard. When I opened my eyes, he was tearing the condom wrapper with his teeth before he put it on. His chest was moving as if he'd run a marathon. His cock was fully erect and ready for action.

"Are you ready?" Sean watched me, waiting for my consent.

"Yes," I murmured.

"How long has it been since you've been with anyone?"

"Almost a year."

"I'll go slow. Stop me if it's too much."

I nodded, and he lowered his body onto mine, fitting perfectly between my legs. Holding himself up on his elbows, he cupped my face and ravished my mouth once again. Switching his weight to one elbow, he trailed his right hand down to my core as his mouth traveled to my breast. The feel of his tongue playing with my breast and his fingers inside my core caused my excitement to build. Both our bodies undulated against each other. Our breaths coming in fast. He gave my other breast the same attention before slowly entering my body.

I felt stretched and a little pain, but I didn't want him to stop. Once he was completely inside me, he halted, giving me a moment to get used to his size. I saw his arms shake, the muscles twitching beneath his skin, visibly fighting to maintain his composure and not hurt me. I glanced up into his face. His eyes were shut, and the tense set of his jaw, his gritted teeth, spoke volumes. Beads of sweat ran down his forehead.

"Hey." I cupped his jaw, and he opened his eyes. "I'm okay. You can move now."

Sean grunted and moved his hips into me. He started slowly, but soon we were both thrusting toward one another. The need was so great I couldn't stop my body from seeking his. An intense rush of euphoria ran through my body, and I dug my nails into his shoulders as my body climaxed. Sean pumped a few more times, then ground his cock into me as his orgasm crested.

Dropping on top of me, he kissed me, then rolled us both so I could lie on his chest. Our hearts pounding wildly as he ran his hands over my back, holding me close.

"That was amazing," he sighed into my hair. "You are amazing."

I chuckled. "You're not so bad yourself."

"Stay with me tonight?" Sean cupped my jaw and raised my face to his.

"On this tiny bed?" I cocked my eyebrow.

"We fit just fine." Sean kissed my forehead. "Besides, with this tiny bed, you can't roll away from me and I can hold you all night." Sean pulled my thigh up to his waist. "Except when I take you again."

"I thought you only had one condom." I kissed his chin.

"Fuck." Sean sighed. "You're right. But we can do other naughty things to each other."

Sean kissed me and slid his finger into my core. We spent the entire night exploring each other's bodies.

Chapter 16

# Unacceptable

## Elias

*Why is she doing this to us?* Doesn't she realize that I'm not okay with sharing? I've been nice to her all week after my coffee issue on Monday. She doesn't need to make me jealous. I'll just have to get her alone and explain things to her. It was bad enough when I caught her eating with him and flirting, but now she's luring him into the house. Where the hell are they going?

I bolted from behind the tree in the park and ran up to the house. Placing my back against the wall, I looked around to make sure no one saw me. I snuck around the house under the cover of night and peeked in every window, looking for Cassie. The only light that was turned on so far was the living room. A light came on in a room and I scurried over to it. That man had Cassie up against the wall and was kissing her.

I needed to find a way inside to stop that man from mauling her. But I saw that man in his Haven Island PD uniform one morning at the coffee shop, which meant he had a gun somewhere in the house. I needed to be smart. I wasn't armed. If I broke in, he might kill me. I needed to get her alone.

A car drove past the house, the headlights shining in my direction as I dove to the ground, lying flat on my stomach. As soon as the car passed, I stood and looked in the window, but they were gone. I checked the windows again and finally found them naked on a narrow bed. He was between her legs and she was enjoying it.

I could do that for her, Mother taught me. If she'd told me she liked that, I would've done it for her already. I watched to see what else she liked so that when she was with me, I could bring her more pleasure than the cop. Feeling a mix of arousal and repulsion, I couldn't resist pleasuring myself while observing her.

I finished myself off at the same time they did. Soon, my pretty Cassie. You'll soon be wearing that expression because of me.

# Chapter 17

# Moving Day

## Sean

Cassie had been sleeping at my new house for the past two nights. I shouldn't have called it sleeping; we made love far more than we slept and I loved every minute. She left early this morning to open the coffee shop. I knew I wouldn't see her until later tonight since she had to work at the restaurant. I told her my stuff was coming on a moving truck from South Florida, so I'd be home all day.

She said she would stop by after work and I promised to make her dinner. She'd only been gone an hour, and I already missed her. Shit, I was falling fucking fast for this girl. It was going to be a long day if I kept pining for her. Deciding to get going, I put on a pair of running shorts and ran along the shoreline. It was another beautiful day in paradise. I ran my usual ten miles in an hour. I was grateful the sand was firm, as loose sand would have made my run much longer; that's why I usually only ran four miles on the beach down south and the remaining six on the road.

I showered and berated myself for not doing a shorter run so I could've driven to the café and gotten a cup of coffee from my beautiful girlfriend. Too late now that I was within the timeframe of delivery the movers gave me. The last thing I wanted was for the truck to arrive, and I wasn't there. Searching the kitchen, I found an old coffee pot and a container of coffee. Thank you, Widow Mary. I made a pot and sat outside, leaving the sliding door open so I could hear the doorbell when they arrived.

Staring at the ocean, I thought about the day I played in the water with Cassie. It was the perfect day. I wanted to make more of those here in my piece of the ocean. We wouldn't have total privacy, but it was only a few steps from the water to my house.

The ringing of the doorbell snapped me out of my thoughts. Jogging to the door, I answered it. The movers were on time.

"Hey, guys."

"Hello, Mr. O'Reilly. I'm Jim. We're ready to unload. Just tell us where you want everything."

"Sounds good, Jim. I'm gonna help. I can't just sit around and let you guys have all the fun."

"Alright, then. Let's get this show on the road." Jim turned and headed to the truck. "Hey, Andy." Jim called out to his moving partner. "Mr. O'Reilly is gonna help us unload."

"Please, call me Sean." I shook Andy's hand.

"Good to meet you."

After introductions, Jim opened the back of the truck and they began carrying the stuff in. For the first time, I appreciated Kerri taking most of our things. They worked fast, emptying the truck. I ordered pizzas for them before Jim and Andy headed back south.

Once they left, I began with the kitchen. Since Widow Mary had left some items, I needed to choose between what I brought and what she left. I was halfway done when the doorbell rang. Checking the time, I saw it was a quarter after three. Had Cassie gotten off work early? I headed to the door, ready to welcome her home.

My smile died on my lips when I opened the door to Kerri. "What the hell are you doing here?"

My sister jumped from beside the door in front of Kerri. "Surprise!"

"Lynn, what are you doing here with Kerri?" I looked between them. They'd never been the best of friends, and I wasn't sure what the hell was going on.

"Well, Kerri said you guys had a misunderstanding. She wanted to apologize, but didn't know where you lived. So, I came with her. Besides, I wanted to see my big brother. I've missed you."

"I've missed you too, squirt." I grabbed my sister and spun her around in a big hug and I wondered what fucking bullshit Kerri had fed her. "Lynn, why don't you go inside? I have some pizza left over in the fridge. I need to talk to Kerri for a minute.

"Okay, thanks."

I waited until Lynn was out of earshot. I stepped out and shut the door. "What the fuck did you tell my sister, and why the hell are you here?"

Kerri reached out and touched my shoulder. I shrugged her arm off me.

"I...I told her the truth. We had a misunderstanding, and I wanted to apologize. I miss you, Sean."

"We did not have a misunderstanding. I caught you fucking another man in our bed and I broke up with you. I don't give a shit that you want to apologize. I told you I never wanted to see you again, and the fact that you lied to my sister to find out where I live is fucking icing on the cake." Placing my hands on my hips, I took several deep breaths, and fought back the urge to strangle her; the prospect of life imprisonment wasn't appealing.

"I'm sorry, okay." Kerri threw her hands up and crossed her arms. "I made a mistake. I don't want to live without you."

"You should have thought about that before you cheated."

"Are you ever going to forgive me?" Kerri's eyes watered.

"You know what? Your tears don't work on me anymore, and I don't have time for this shit." I pointed to the door behind me. "I'm gonna go inside and hang out with my sister. I don't give a shit what you do."

I turned away from Kerri and went inside.

"Hey, you ever hear of eating at a table?" I gave Lynn shit before I sat on my favorite recliner.

"I wanted to use your kitchen table, but it was covered in boxes," Lynn explained, eating.

"Well, that's true. So, tell me how you've been." I leaned back in my recliner and saw Kerri come in and sit next to her on the couch.

"Have a slice, Kerri." Lynn pointed toward the box.

"Thank you. That's so sweet of you to offer." Kerri grabbed a slice.

"You two make up?" Lynn winked at me.

"We still need to talk...," I cut Kerri off.

"We are not dating anymore, Lynn. I'm sorry you made the trip all the way up here to hear that, but I am glad to see you." I glared at Kerri, daring her to correct me.

"Why not?" Lynn looked surprised by my comment. "I mean, she came all the way up here. Don't you think you should give her a chance?"

I was shocked that Kerri had involved Lynn. I really didn't want to tell my thirteen-year-old sister what Kerri had done.

"It's between us." I pointed between Kerri and me. "Please, let it go."

"Can we talk on the back porch for a minute, Sean?" Kerri stood and walked to the sliding glass door.

"Sure." I smiled at Lynn and followed Kerri outside.

To avoid being overheard by Lynn, I lowered my voice and stood with my back to the house. My anger toward Kerri was something my sister didn't need to see.

"Why are you doing this?" I said through gritted teeth at Kerri. "You need to let this go. My sister is too young to hear the gory details of what you did. She doesn't need to know how vindictive you are."

"I think we can work this out." Kerri stepped close to me and put her hands on my shoulders.

I raised my hands and grabbed her wrists, ready to pull them off, when she leaned into me and planted a kiss on my lips. I wasn't expecting it, but the worst part was the loud gasp I heard from the side of the house. I pulled my head back and saw Cassie's face drain of color. She dropped the bag of food she had been holding and covered her mouth.

"Cassie, this isn't what you think." I tried to push Kerri away, but she grabbed onto my shirt and pulled me off balance. I crashed with Kerri onto the table. When I looked up, Cassie was gone.

"Get the fuck away from me!" I hollered at Kerri and shoved her hands off me.

Running around the house, I saw Cassie jump into her car and start it. I ran to the driver's side door and pulled on the door handle, but it was locked.

"Cassie, wait!" I screamed and banged on the window. She jolted in her seat and turned to me. Tears running down her face.

"How could you?" She yelled before she put her car in reverse and backed up, forcing me to jump away from the car or get my foot run over.

"Cassie, please!" I begged, but it didn't matter. She glared at me and gunned her car as soon as she cleared my driveway.

I had to follow her. I needed to explain. But, I couldn't leave my sister alone. I stormed back into the house and saw my sister comforting Kerri on the couch. Fuck no, this was ending right the fuck now.

"Kerri, I think you need to leave."

"Sean, how could you be so mean to her?" Lynn screamed at me.

"How could I be mean to her?" I pointed to myself, baffled by my sister's comment. "I wasn't the one who cheated on her."

"You cheated on Sean?" Lynn's head bounced between us like a spectator at a tennis match. "Kerri, you said he was mad at you because he didn't want to get rid of the recliner. Not because you cheated on him."

"Lynn, you need to stay out of this." I pointed to my sister. "And Kerri, you need to leave now."

"But Sean." Kerri flat out ignored Lynn and pouted like she used to when we were dating and I would do anything she asked.

"That look won't work on me anymore. Not after what you did." I was pacing, trying to figure out why she wasn't with Thad. Wait a minute. Thad must've dumped her, and she didn't want to be alone. I spun around and faced Kerri. "Did Thad dump you? Did you cheat on him too? Is that why you're here?"

"I'm no longer seeing Thad because I missed you." Kerri took a couple of steps toward me.

"Never touch me again." I pointed to my front door. "My girlfriend peeled out of here because she thinks I cheated on her with you. Get the fuck out of my house so I can explain to her how my toxic ex-girlfriend is fucking crazy and the kiss she saw meant nothing to me."

"Well, fuck you, Sean!" Kerri turned into her natural born selfish bitch and stormed out of my house.

I followed my sister out the front door as she ran after Kerri.

"Kerri, wait. How will I get home?" Lynn hollered.

Kerri rolled down her window and sarcastically said, "Let your fucking brother drive your ass home. It's not like you helped me. Worthless O'Reilly's!" she hollered before she screeched her tires, pulling out of my driveway.

Lynn whispered and ran into my arms and whispered, "I'm sorry."

"It's okay." I ran my hand over the back of her head. "She had me fooled too when I dated her."

"She was so nice to me on the way here." Lynn's tears soaked my shirt. "How will I get home?"

"Hey." I lifted her face and wiped her tears. "I'll drive you home, squirt. It's gonna be okay." Lynn had idolized Kerri while we dated, since her mother was always out. This was a hard fall for Lynn to take, realizing that Kerri wasn't who she thought she was for the past couple of years.

"I feel bad for trying to get you guys together. I didn't know she cheated. Do you forgive me?"

"Nothing to forgive." I pulled her in for a tight hug. "You didn't know the whole story."

"Yeah." Lynn sighed. "Can you do me a favor?"

"Sure, what do you need?" I pulled her away from me and looked down at her.

"Can you go take a shower?" Lynn used her fingers to close her nose. "You stink."

"You little shit, be nice to me if you want me to give you a ride home. Otherwise, I'll send you back on a bus with strangers." I gave her a noogie.

"Hey, stop that. You know I hate that. It knots my hair." Lynn pulled away from me and swatted my hand. "You would never put me on a bus alone." Lynn rolled her eyes at my empty threat and went back into the house.

I chuckled. She was right. I would never endanger her safety. "I'll be right there. I just need to make a quick phone call."

"To your girlfriend?" Lynn stopped in the hallway and faced me.

"Yeah," I sighed. "She looked hurt. I need her to know that I care about her and not Kerri." I pulled the phone from my back pocket. "I'll be there in a minute."

"Take your time. And while you're at it, apologize to her for my bringing the crazy lady to your house."

I smiled. "I will."

I dialed Cassie's number. She should be home by now, but she never answered. It just went straight to voicemail, so I left her a message.

*Cass, it's me. What you saw wasn't what you think. I want to talk to you. Please call me and let me explain.*

Then I texted her, hoping she would see that and answer me.

> Sean: What you saw didn't mean anything. Please call me.

Later that night, I got a text from Cassie.

> Cassie: I've found someone else. You need to leave me alone.

> Sean: What the fuck? Call me.

I never got another response from Cassie, even though I called and texted several more times. What did she mean she found someone else? That wasn't like her. I got Lynn settled into one of the twin beds and I slept on the full that I brought from home. I needed to buy a bigger bed soon, but for tonight, it would have to do.

Lynn and I agreed to wake up early so I could drive her home. I called my dad and let him know what happened and that I wouldn't be able to stay long. As soon as I delivered Lynn, I would turn around and head back to Haven Island. I had to work on Monday.

Chapter 18

# My Prince Turned into a Toad

## Cassie

The sight of that woman's body pressed against Sean as she kissed him left me in disbelief. Dropping dinner, I ran to my car, heartbroken. How could he treat me like that? When he banged on my window and said she kissed him and not the other way around, I ignored him. Was he telling the truth? Did she kiss him and not the other way around?

Craving ice cream to help me wallow in my misery, I drove to "Yummy Scoops" and got my usual cookies and cream ice cream in a cup; the creamy texture was heavenly. My phone rang as I was ordering. It was Sean. I switched my phone to silent because I wasn't ready to talk yet. I needed time to think about what I'd seen. Instead of answering, I drove to the park.

The park gazebo had always been a relaxing place for me. Seated in the shade, I could still see the ocean and feel the breeze on my face. It was close to Sean's house, and I knew I'd have to face him at some point. It wasn't like me to ignore someone forever.

I parked, then strolled toward the gazebo, enjoying my delicious ice cream and waving to families heading home for dinner. Shoot, dinner. My stomach rumbled at the thought of that juicy burger I dropped on Sean's patio. Oh well, the ice cream would have to do.

Sean kissing that woman was an image seared into my mind as I gazed at the ocean. The more I thought about it, the more apparent it became he wasn't returning the kiss. He pushed her arms back as he leaned his head back. She had forced herself on him.

I wish I had stayed and fought for my man. I betrayed his trust by leaving. Setting my empty cup of ice cream on the bench, I picked up my phone to call Sean. My phone was blowing up with texts and voicemails from Sean. I'd forgotten it was on silent.

"Cassie, how are you?"

Elias startled me by suddenly sitting beside me on the bench; I jumped and dropped my phone. Where had he come from?

"I'm good. How are you?"

"Have you been crying?" Elias handed me a napkin.

"What do you mean?" I wiped my hands over my cheeks. They were dry. How did he know I had been crying?

"You look sad, and your eyes are red."

"Oh," I sighed. "I'm okay."

"Can I get you anything? I know how much you like to read and I just got this new book from your favorite author. Do you want to read it? I can get it out of my car for you."

"No, it's okay."

How did Elias know I liked to read? I never saw him at the café when I took my breaks and sat down with my book. Maybe he saw me exchange books with friends while he was in line waiting for his order?

Looking around, I saw several families leaving, their laughter echoing as the sun dipped below the horizon, painting the sky in warm hues. Soon, the park would be eerily quiet. I shivered, realizing we were alone.

"How do you know who my favorite author is?" Elias was another problem I didn't need right now.

"I've seen you reading."

I stared at him. It must've been a blank stare, because he continued.

"When I get my coffee or eat dinner at the restaurant." Elias sheepishly looked down. "And I asked your sister."

I was gonna have to talk to Kristy about her loose lips. With each passing moment beside Elias, a wave of discomfort washed over me. I needed to go talk to Sean.

I stood. "I gotta go, but it was nice seeing you." It really wasn't, but since he was being nice, I should return the favor.

"I have to go home as well." Elias stood, blocking my exit. "Please let me give you the book. It's her new one and I think you will like it. Come with me and I'll hand it to you before we leave."

"Okay, sure. I'll grab it from you." I put my phone back in my purse and grabbed my empty ice cream cup. There was a trash can on the way where I could toss it. I was grateful for the few light posts that illuminated our way to the parking lot. Since Elias had been nice to me all week, not his previous creepy self. If he had made kind gestures toward me, shouldn't I be nice to him?

The gray car looked familiar, but it was probably from when he came by the café. As we approached the car, he went to the passenger seat and opened the door.

"It's on the seat." He motioned for me to get it.

I leaned down to grab the book. When I felt a pinprick on my neck, I knew I'd made a grave mistake. My world blurred, and I collapsed onto the seat before I blacked out.

# Chapter 19

# Gotcha

## Elias

That had been easier than I thought. When I filled the syringe with the drug from a dealer earlier today, I never expected it to take effect so quickly. Here I was berating myself for not injecting her while we were talking so the drug could work its way into her system, but in the end, I'd chosen the perfect time to administer it. I hope I didn't give her too much. Looking around to make sure no one saw me, I threw her legs into the car and shut the door.

Feeling the urgency, I slammed the car door, the engine's growl vibrating through the car as I raced down main street and crossed the bridge into the mainland. My eyes darted between the road and my mirrors. The sight of her and me in a car on the island would raise a lot of eyebrows—too many prying eyes—but on the mainland, we could disappear.

I drove her to my house. I couldn't wait for Mother to meet her. They would get along well as long as Mother thought Cassie loved me. My story of how Cassie and I met started with some white lies, but I wanted Cassie to make a good first impression.

Cassie was still out when we reached home, so I carefully supported her, slipping her arm around my shoulder and gripping her at the waist. Mother was on the couch, knitting and watching her favorite game show.

"Hello, dear. Who is that with you? Is she okay?" Mother set down her needles.

"Yes, mother. This is my girlfriend, Cassie. She's just a little drunk." I pulled Cassie closer to me.

"Drinking before dinner!" Mother sounded appalled. "What kind of woman does that? Why did you choose her?"

"She didn't mean to Mother, but don't worry. I'm gonna take her to my room to rest. We'll be down in time for dinner."

"Okay, but make sure she's sober. I don't want a drunk woman at our table as we bless our food."

"Yes, mother."

Cassie was rolling her head, beginning to wake up. I needed to get her upstairs so she could listen to reason. Mother and Father had raised me in this modest two-bedroom house, but after the age of eighteen, when Father caught Mother kissing me, he asked for a divorce and kicked us out. We didn't like his tone. Mother grabbed my baseball bat and hit him several times. We buried the body in our backyard under the big shade tree.

Once Father died, Mother and I slept in the same room, but now Mother said I needed to find a younger woman to give her grandkids. That's when I chose Cassie and moved my stuff into the attic because Mother said Cassie wouldn't want to share a bed with us. Especially when we were making babies. Mother taught me how to please a woman and told me it would take a few tries before my seed would become a baby. I was looking forward to trying.

The attic was a good place for us for two good reasons. One, I could lock the door from the outside and keep Cassie from leaving me. Two, if Cassie and I had a fight, Mother wouldn't be able to hear her and get upset. I wanted to do things right, so before I could bed Cassie, I wanted to marry her. Mother had already taken out her wedding dress and had it dry cleaned.

I laid Cassie on my bed and handcuffed one of her hands to the headboard. Mother had told me to do that in case she woke up angry. Dinner wouldn't be ready for another few hours, so I sat in the chair next to the bed and waited for her to wake up. I had nothing better to do, and looking at her beautiful face made me happy.

Cassie began to groan and move around on the bed. I leaned forward and held her other hand. Her body jolted, and she opened her eyes.

"Elias," Cassie whispered and looked around. "Where am I?"

"We are in my room." I smiled.

"What do you mean, your room?"

"My bedroom in Mother's house."

"Why am I here?" Cassie pulled her hand away from mine. Her eyes went wide at the sight of her other hand chained to the headboard. She tugged repeatedly at her handcuffed hand.

"Because we are going to be married." I stood proudly announcing our impending nuptials. "You are going to be my wife and bear my children so Mother can have the grandkids she's been wanting."

Cassie's eyes bulged out of her head like a bad cartoon, and she used her feet to scoot back toward the headboard, wrapping her loose hand around her knees. "What are you talking about?"

Chapter 20

# Where are You?

## Sean

I still hadn't heard from Cassie after she blew me off, but I had to get Lynn home. After showering, I went into the spare bedroom and woke Lynn.

Sitting on the edge of the bed, I nudged her awake. "It's time to get up. We gotta go, so I have enough time to drive back."

"So, you can fix things with your girlfriend," Lynn mumbled.

"Yep, so let's roll. We're burning daylight hours." I stood. "We'll go to a drive-thru and I'll get you breakfast, but only if you get up and are ready to go within the next ten minutes."

"Okay, okay." Lynn got up and headed straight to the bathroom.

As I waited for Lynn, I paced my living room. I was eager to get back and find Cassie. I couldn't remember if she told me she worked today. Pulling out my phone, I was ready to dial the café when I heard Lynn's voice.

"I'm ready."

I'd call later. We left and stopped at a drive-thru as promised. I tried the radio to distract me from my thoughts, but in the end, I preferred to talk to my sister.

"When's your last day of school?"

"Next week." Lynn munched on her donut.

"What are your plans for this summer?" I usually kept up with the family's vacation plans, even though most of the time I couldn't go. Kerri always found excuses to avoid spending our vacations with my family. She always said we spent enough time with them during the week and our vacations were for me to dote on her.

"Mom, Dad, and I are going camping."

"Where are you guys going?"

"Dad said he wanted to go to Yellowstone and sleep in a tent. Mom wants to stay in a hotel, but dad says we need to experience it like the old days." Lynn took a sip of her juice.

"So, what you're saying is that you guys are going glamping at Yellowstone." I grinned at her. I knew there was no way in hell Cheryl would stay in a tent.

"Yep." Lynn grinned back. "Mom always wins the sleeping arrangement battle whenever Dad picks a vacation spot. He can't say no to her."

I knew that. My father devoted himself to his wife. He was a wonderful husband to my mother, showering her with love and attention, and later to Cheryl, but his role as a father was sadly lacking. He always put his wives and his job above his kids. Which was fine. I was used to it. My sister told me about all the fun things planned for their trip.

I made small comments here and there, but my mind kept wandering to Cassie. I hated having an argument between us. As soon as I got back to Haven Island, I was going to find her and sit her ass down. She was not leaving until she heard my side.

Bursting from the car as we pulled up to my dad's, Lynn raced to the front door, unlocked it, and yelled, "Mom! Dad! I'm back."

Dad came out of his study, which was now his man cave since retirement. He traded his old wooden desk for recliners and a big-screen TV to watch sports.

"Hey," he smiled and hugged Lynn. "How did it go? Where's Kerri?"

"Don't ask," Lynn mumbled against my dad's chest. "Taking her to Sean was a huge mistake. She's such a bitch."

"Watch your language, young lady," Cheryl said from behind my dad. "It's good to see you, Sean." Cheryl gave me a quick hug.

Lynn pulled away from dad and hugged Cheryl. "It was horrible, Mom," Lynn said as she pulled Cheryl with her into the kitchen.

"It didn't go well, huh?" Dad hugged me.

"Why did you let Lynn bring her? You knew what happened. There was no way in hell I would ever take Kerri back." My dad knew the story. I had told him one night over dinner.

"I'm sorry." He bowed his head and shook it. "Kerri sounded so convincing. I thought she should tell you what she was telling me about how sorry she was and how she missed being a part of our family."

"She's a lying bitch." I placed my hands on my hips and took a deep breath. "Please, stay out of it from now on and, for God's sake, do not listen to her lies."

"I won't. I promise." Dad held up his hand and nodded. "How about some lunch? Cheryl ordered some sandwiches from that place you like. We can eat them out by the pool."

Dad looked so hopeful as he studied my reaction.

"Sure. I could use a quick break from driving."

"Great." Dad slapped my back and smiled.

"But as soon as we're done, I gotta head out." I said sternly. I didn't want him thinking I had time to hang around and watch sports. I still had another four hours home and time with Cassie.

I followed my dad outside. Cheryl and Lynn had already brought everything to the table and were talking about their trip. Cheryl was excited to let me know dad had spared no expense on this trip. They were going first class all the way. I glanced at my dad, but he just sat there smiling at Cheryl.

"We wish you could come with us?" Cheryl placed her hand over my dads on the table. "I know your father would love that."

"I appreciate the offer, but with this new job, I can't take time off right now. It sounds like you guys will have a great time."

"I wish you were coming," Lynn sighed.

"I'll miss you, squirt." I ruffled Lynn's hair and watched her glare at me as she finger combed it back in place. She hated when I did that. "Take lots of photos and I'll come down one weekend so you can show them to me."

"Okay." Lynn picked up her sandwich and took a big bite.

When we finished, I knew dad would ask me to stay.

"Sean, you want to watch a few minutes of a game with me?"

"Lynn." Cheryl stood and wiped her mouth with a napkin. "Clear the table and put the dishes in the dishwasher. I'm meeting some friends for some shopping." Cheryl walked behind my dad and draped her arms over him, kissing his cheek. "I want to get some items for our camping trip."

My dad held her hand and brought it to his lips for a kiss. "Have fun, honey."

"See you all later." Cheryl waved her fingers and left.

"So, can you stay for a few minutes?" Dad got up and helped clear the table with Lynn.

Shit, I was going to get home later than I thought. "Sure, maybe an hour."

"I'll take what I can get."

I helped Lynn load the dishwasher before I headed to the man cave. When my dad looked at me, he seemed sad. If all his days were like this, I wondered how much time he spent with Cheryl. Maybe I could get him to talk to me. Throughout his marriage with Cheryl, my dad never challenged her financial decisions. He would be lucky if she didn't run through his pension before he died. But that was his life, and I wasn't getting in the middle of it. I had tried once. He didn't speak to me for several months, which was fine with me, but then Cheryl wouldn't let me hang out with Lynn. So, I apologized to both of them and kept my mouth shut so my relationship with Lynn could continue and I could be there for her if she ever needed me.

My mom and I were closer when I was a child because of my dad's work schedule. After mom died and dad married Cheryl, dad and I became even more distant. Then Lynn was born. She became the heart of our family, causing me to build a better relationship with my dad and Cheryl.

I sat with dad for about an hour before I left. Needing to talk to my best friend on my drive back to the island, I called George.

"Hey, how's it going? Did the moving truck arrive yesterday?" George sounded happy.

"Yeah, it did and so did Kerri."

"What the fuck! How did she know where you were? I swear I didn't tell her shit."

I smiled. Kerri had tried to talk to George after the breakup, but he avoided her like the plague and would tell me every time she called.

"I know you didn't. She buttered up my sister. Lynn came with her."

"Holy Fuck! That had to suck. What happened?"

I gave George the rundown. He was well aware of Kerri and her deceitful lies.

"Shit, man. You gotta find Cassie and explain everything. If you need me to talk to her, I'll back you up. I know all about Kerri's shit."

"Thanks. I might take you up on that. How are you and Lizzy?"

"We're good. Just finished eating brunch and we're sitting by the pool at the resort." George's voice sounded further away when he said, "Hey guys, it's Sean. Say hi."

Sean smiled as he heard several voices at once saying hello to him and telling him they wished he was there.

"I guess the gang's all there, huh?"

George chuckled. "Everyone except Thunder, Isa, and Thomas. Thomas is still too little and Isa's exhausted."

"Hey, old man." Sean smiled when he heard Tim's voice. "I miss beating you on the court."

"Yeah, I bet you do. How are you, Tim?" Tim was the oldest in the shelter home for boys where George and I volunteered.

"Doing great. I graduated and will start the police academy in the fall."

George had grown up in that home and when he became my partner, I met all those boys. It didn't take long for those boys to grow on me and I became a mentor like George. Several times a week, George and I helped them with their homework or took them to the park to play basketball. I missed them. Maybe I could find some kids to mentor on Haven Island.

"I'm so damn proud of you." I told Tim.

"Thanks, man. I gotta go show these youngun's how to do a proper cannon ball. Miss you."

"Now, who's the old man?" Sean heard Tim laugh followed by a splash and a female voice saying, "Tim, do not be jumping when the pool is full." That sounded like Freya, Holt's girlfriend.

George's laughter came over the line. "We miss you, man. Keep me updated on Cassie."

"I will. Thanks, I miss you all too."

I hung up the phone and blasted my radio for my last hour of the drive. An hour was a piece of cake compared to the previous seven I had already spent in my car today. Don't get me wrong, I loved my car, and I didn't mind driving, but I was dying to see Cassie. I drove straight to Hi Grill. If she was going to break up with me, I wanted her to do it to my face. But I hoped we could kiss and make up. I missed not waking up next to her.

Chapter 21

# House of Terror

## Cassie

T hough awake, I feigned sleep, replaying the previous night's terrifying dinner in my mind. Once seated, Elias' mother sat at the head of the table as Elias served dinner.

*"You will stop drinking now that you are marrying my son," Mother said to me.*

*"I'm not marrying your son." I said calmly.*

*She stood and slapped me so hard on the* face; *I fell out of my chair.*

*"Mother, what have you done?" Elias put down the dishes and ran to me. Helping me sit on the chair.*

*I pushed him and bolted out of the chair. In a desperate attempt to escape, I scrambled towards the heavy oak front door, its multiple bolts and locks resisting my frantic efforts. Suddenly, a sharp blow to my arm sent me crashing to the floor. Hot tears streamed down my face, each drop burning like the fire that shot up my shoulders. With a gasp, I grabbed my arm, my heart pounding, and looked behind me. Mother stood beside Elias, a baseball bat clutched in her hand, ready for anything.*

*"Do that again and I'll kill you? Do you hear me? You will not speak to me like that. You will marry my son, and you will bear his children. Stop your quivering and get back to the table so we can bless our food and eat like a family!"*

*Mother's harsh words petrified me; her voice still echoed in my ears. Those people were not stable. I stumbled to my feet, clutching my throbbing arm, wondering if she'd broken something; the pain was sharp and insistent. Elias tried to help me, but I took a step back.*

*Mother glared at me, so I sucked it up and accepted his help. If I was going to make it out of here alive, I had to play along until either someone would find me or I could escape.*

*After we sat down, Mother said. "Elias, cuff her to the chair so she doesn't do anything stupid again."*

*"Yes, Mother."*

*Elias got up and tightly zip tied my left wrist to the leg of the chair. After he sat down, he raised his hands in prayer form and looked at Mother. She nodded and glared at me. I couldn't lift my left hand, but put my right hand up as if to pray. Mother smirked at me before she closed her eyes and bowed her head.*

*"Lord, bless this food and the union between my son and his chosen bride. May she be very fertile and bring me many grandchildren to raise like I raised my beautiful son." Mother leaned toward Elias and kissed him full on the lips.*

*I looked up and froze. Holy shit, this was incest and creepy as hell.*

*"Amen." Both Elias and Mother murmured against each other's lips before they smiled at each other and began eating.*

*I didn't know what to say, so I had stayed quiet and ate my food, hoping it wasn't poisoned. Then again, they needed me alive to bear all his children. What the hell had I gotten myself into for a fucking book and to be nice to a creepy guy?*

*I had stayed silent throughout the meal. I answered when spoken to, but otherwise just listened to their conversation. They spoke to each other like lovers, asking about their day and how much they missed each other. I came to realize I was just a vessel for their spawn. I was not about to get pregnant by this crazy man. Getting away from him would be easier than Mother. She was evil incarnate.*

*After dinner, Mother went to get her wedding dress and brought it back on a hanger.*

*"This is the dress you will wear. I wore it when I wed his father and you will wear it to wed Elias."*

*"I mean no disrespect, but I don't think it's my size?" The dress looked to be larger than a size twelve and I wore a size two.*

*"You will wear this dress!" Mother shouted and placed her hand on the bat.*

*"Mother," Elias spoke up. "Maybe you can fix it for her since you are a whiz with a sewing machine?"*

*"That's a good idea." Mother beamed at Elias. "You are so smart." She bent down and kissed him again.*

*Ew, that was so* gross. *I looked down at my plate.*

*"We will start tomorrow. I think it will take me a few days to fit it properly. When I'm done, we'll get a justice of the peace to come over and you can marry under the tree in the backyard so your father can be present even though he was a horrible man."*

*I looked up at them. "Your father died, Elias?" I asked. I hadn't seen a father, but I wasn't sure if maybe he was away for work.*

*"I killed him because he didn't accept our love. Right, my love." Mother placed her hand on Elias' shoulder.*

*"Yes, Mother."*

*Oh, hell no! Now I was panicking inside. I scooted my chair back and asked to be excused. Asking for ibuprofen to dull the pain, Mother gave me two and told Elias to escort me to the bedroom while she cleaned up.*

As I lay thinking about everything that happened, I looked at my cuffed arm that was still throbbing and turning black and blue. Closing my eyes, I prayed someone would realize I was missing, especially now that I missed my morning shift at the café.

"Mother and I are going to church."

My body jolted, and I opened my eyes. I must have been so deep into my thoughts that I didn't hear Elias come in until he spoke up.

"She doesn't think you are ready to be nice in public, so we are going to leave you here." Elias ran a hand down my face, and I cringed. My face was still sore from his slap. "You need to learn to be nice to Mother. You won't like the consequences if you don't do what she says."

"Did she do something to you? Elias, we can leave here together. I can help you." I thought maybe he was here under duress and his love for me could pull him away so he could seek help, and I could go home.

Elias blinked and smiled. "I'm crazy about you, Cassie, but I could never leave Mother alone. I love her."

Elias got up to leave.

"Can I please use the restroom before you leave?"

"Of course." Elias uncuffed me from the headboard. I rubbed my wrist, then held my arm as I walked into the bathroom. After using the restroom, I stood on the toilet to reach for the window, only to discover it was firmly sealed shut. I didn't escape because I thought it might be best if I tried after they left.

After I finished, he cuffed me again to the headboard and left. I sat up in bed and pulled on the headboard. The pain was excruciating, a searing, white-hot agony that made me want to scream, but my will to escape was stronger. If I could break the slats, I could slide the cuffs off and use the broken slat as a weapon. That would be my best shot at escaping this house of horrors.

## Chapter 22

# Stalker Took My Girl

## Sean

The door to Hi Grill jingled when I opened it. I scanned the room for Cass, but didn't see her. Judy walked up to me with a puzzled look on her face.

"Hi, Sean. Where's Cassie? I thought she was with you."

"What do you mean?" My heart started racing.

"I haven't seen her since she left with dinner for both of you yesterday."

"We...uh, we," I stuttered. I never stuttered. I rubbed the back of my neck and grew some balls. "We had an argument. She saw something that wasn't what it seemed and stormed out. I've been calling and texting, but she won't answer. I thought she was here and I could talk to her."

"What took you so long to come talk to her?" Judy crossed her arms and glared at him.

"I had to drive my sister home to South Florida, and I just got back." I could feel myself sweating under the glare of Judy's eyes. I looked into the kitchen and saw Carl put the spatula down and head toward me.

"Did she think your sister was a girlfriend?" Judy inquired.

"Uh, no." I chuckled and rubbed my chin. She was going to be royally pissed at me when I told her what happened. "My sister is only thirteen. But she saw my ex kiss me and thought I was with her."

I could see the anger rising in Judy's face just as Carl approached us.

"What the hell is going on? Where's Cassie?" He put his arm around his wife.

"I was hoping she was here." I looked around again. Were they lying to me? Did she still not want to talk to me?

"She's not. After what you did, do you think she would want to talk to you even if she was?" Judy glared at me.

"I didn't kiss my ex. She kissed me." I was freaking out. The last thing I wanted was for her parents to hate me. "I was trying to push her away. I ran after Cassie trying to explain, but she peeled out of my driveway and she hasn't spoken to me since."

"You broke her heart!" Judy yelled at me and pointed at my face.

"I know." I sighed and bowed my head before I looked at her. "I didn't mean to. I want to apologize and explain everything. Do you know where she is?"

"No." Judy relaxed her shoulders and stopped glaring at me. "But I know she didn't come home last night, and she didn't show up for work at the café." A look of horror came over Judy, and she covered her mouth. "Oh, my God. If she wasn't with you last night, where did she go?"

"I don't know." I thought I was worried before, but nothing like the panic that set in when I realized no one knew where Cassie was. It was time to think like a cop instead of a lovesick fool. "Where does Cassie usually go when she wants to think about something?"

"The gazebo at the park," Carl spoke up as he hugged Judy.

"Okay, I'll go check it out."

"Please, call us if you find her," Carl croaked.

"What's going on here?" Chief Reyes came over.

I'd seen him at a table with his son and what looked to be his parents, but didn't want to interrupt.

"Cassie's missing." I blurted.

"What do you mean, missing?" Chief Reyes glanced between all of them.

I summarized the story for him because we were losing time and all I wanted to do was go to the park and see if Cassie was there. Although, I couldn't imagine her sleeping there.

"I'll follow you to the park. I just have to let my parents know to take Holden home with them."

"Okay, thanks." I waved and ran to my car.

The trip to the park, which was only a few miles, felt like hours. When I pulled in, I saw her car. Oh, thank God. Relief swept over me as I got out. I tried her car door, but it remained locked. Glancing inside, I didn't see her. I looked around and didn't see her nearby. The hood of her car was cold. Her car had been here awhile. I headed to the gazebo but didn't see her. My search of the shoreline proved fruitless; Cassie was nowhere in sight.

As I headed back to the gazebo, I saw Chief Reyes waiting for me.

"Did you find her?" he asked.

"No, I don't see her anywhere, but her car is still here, and the hood is cold."

"Where the hell could she be?" Chief Reyes pointed to the closest house to the park. "Let's go knock on their door and see if they saw Cassie."

I let the chief knock. He wasn't in uniform, but everyone knew him.

"Hi, Chief." A lady answered the door. "What's going on?"

Her son came running to the door. He must've heard her. "Hi, Chief Reyes!" he screeched before he dove into the chief's arms.

"Hi, Abby. Hey, Adam." The chief hugged Adam and stepped back. "Have either of you seen Cassie Fulton?"

"I haven't. I'm sorry." Abby put her arm around her son as he stood in front of her.

"I saw her yesterday." Adam, who looked to be around eight years old, shouted. "She was at the park with a man."

"Did you recognize the man?" Chief Reyes crouched down to his level.

"No." Adam shrugged.

"Can you tell me what he looked like?"

"He was a little taller than Cassie. Not as tall as you." Adam pointed at the chief. "Brown hair parted to the side, longer in the front than in the back and skinny."

"Is there anything else you remember? Maybe a tattoo or what he was wearing?"

"I wasn't close enough to see any tattoos, but he had on clothes like my dad wears for work."

The chief and I both glanced at Abby.

"Ken wears a white button down and dress pants to work." Abby looked down at her son. "Is that what you mean, Adam?"

"Yep, that's it."

"What did you see them doing? Were they in the gazebo, sitting on the park bench, playing on the slide, or climbing the monkey bars?" Chief Reyes smiled at Adam.

"No, that's silly. Adults don't use our slide or monkey bars." Adam laughed. "I saw them walking to his car, but then mom called me and I came inside to eat dinner."

"Do you remember the color or type of car?"

"It was a gray. I don't know much about cars."

"Okay, thanks, Adam." Chief Reyes gave him a high five. "You've been a big help." Chief Reyes stood. "Can I talk to your mom for a second?"

"Sure. Bye." Adam ran back into the house.

While the chief was talking to Adam, I had scanned the outside of the house and saw a camera that faced the park. After Adam ran in, I elbowed the chief and pointed toward it.

"Abby, is that camera working?" Chief Reyes nodded to the camera by her front porch.

"Yes. Ken installed it after those kids were caught smoking in the park and causing trouble to the houses nearby. Come inside. I'll show you the footage."

I couldn't wait to see who Cassie was with because maybe her text that she found someone else was right. My heart felt shattered even though I'd only known her a week. She was Mrs. Right, but apparently I was Mr. Not Right Now. Feeling like I was going to the gallows, I strolled through Abby's house into an office.

She pulled up the footage on a computer. "We have two more cameras on the side of the house, so you'll get a view of the parking lot, the gazebo, and the playground.

"Can you go back to...," Chief Reyes turned to me, "about what time, Sean?"

"Can you start at four?" That was around the time Cassie saw me with Kerri.

Abby fast-forwarded until we saw Cassie appear on one screen, carrying a bowl of ice cream. We watched her sit in the gazebo and stare toward the ocean.

"Keep going forward until we see a man approach her." Chief Reyes murmured.

Cassie sat so long that the sun went down, leaving her alone where parents and children had been. Then a man showed up, walking to the gazebo. I couldn't see his face to be sure, but he looked familiar. He entered the gazebo and startled Cassie. They talked for a bit, then they headed to the parking lot.

"Can you zoom in on his face?" Chief Reyes and I both leaned toward the screen.

It was a little fuzzy, but I said, "That's Elias," at the same time Chief Reyes said, "That's the creepy guy that was watching her at the restaurant the other day. Let it play out so we can see what happened."

I braced myself for what I was about to watch. There was no way she would go with him willingly anywhere. He opened his passenger door and pointed inside. We saw Cassie lean in and then his arm moved toward her back and she collapsed.

"What the hell!" I screamed, forgetting there was a small child in the house.

"Abby, zoom in again, please." Chief Reyes glanced at me. "Watch your language."

"Don't worry about Adam. He's in his room watching cartoons. He can't hear you." Abby zoomed in.

"Is that a syringe he took out of his pocket?" I stared in shock at what I was seeing. He'd drugged her.

"Yeah, looks like it." Chief Reyes rubbed his jaw.

Then the asshole grabbed her legs and shoved her into his car before he drove off. My girl had been abducted, and I didn't know shit about this town or where to look.

"Abby, can you please make a copy of this and put it on a flash drive for me?"

"Absolutely." Abby hurried to find a flash drive, put it in, copied the file, and handed it to the chief. "I'm so sorry. I hope you find her."

"Thanks Abby. We appreciate all your help."

Where was she? What had he done to her? She'd been gone almost twenty-four hours now. My eyes were tearing up as I saw Cassie's beautiful smile in my mind. Was that how I was going to remember her, or was it seeing her body collapsing in that fucking asshole's car? Then I felt a shove to my shoulder. "Snap out of it. We need to find Cassie–now."

I blinked and cleared my throat. Nodding, I thanked Abby and followed the chief outside.

"Let's go to the station and put out a BOLO (Be On the Lookout) and CLEAR (Coordinated Law Enforcement Adult Rescue) Alert for Cassie and her abductor."

"I'll be there in a minute. I need to go talk to Cassie's parents. I promised them an update."

"Okay." Chief Reyes squeezed my shoulder. "I can see that you love Cassie. Hang in there, we'll find her."

"Thanks."

I got into my car and drove to the restaurant. My adrenaline wanted me to go straight to the police station or drive around looking for her, but I knew I needed to tell Judy and Carl what had happened. It was my fault she had run from me into the arms of a killer. After I parked, before I even stepped one foot out of my car, I looked up and Cassie's parents were holding each other, standing at the front door staring at me. This was gonna suck balls.

Chapter 23

# No Way Out

## Cassie

I waited for the sound of the front door closing after Elias left, but I couldn't hear a thing from the attic. For a good ten minutes, I watched the clock on the wall before I rolled over and started kicking the bed slats. My foot throbbed, a crimson stain blooming on the pale skin where I'd kicked the headboard barefoot. That first night, Elias took my shoes, and I couldn't see them from the bed.

The slat finally snapped off the headboard, and the momentum sent me flying into the remaining slats. The blow to my head momentarily stunned me, but after a couple of deep breaths, I slid the cuffs off the broken slat. I gripped the broken piece of slat, yanking it free from the headboard. I'd need a weapon to defend myself against Elias and Mother.

I checked the windows, but they were all sealed shut. A couple of kids riding by on their bikes were so caught up in their conversation that they didn't notice me banging and screaming at the window. I tried to break the window with the slat when the kids were in front of the house, but the slat snapped. Shit! Looking left and right, I didn't see anyone else outside, only well-kept lawns that complemented the middle-class homes. The boys that rode by looked like normal little boys having fun, not psychopaths. It's unbelievable that the neighbors were unaware of the two lunatics living nearby.

Frantically, I scanned the room, searching for a sturdy object to shatter the glass and escape through a second-story window. At this point, I didn't care if I ended up with a broken leg from my reckless jump; the adrenaline coursing through me, the thump-thump-thump of my heart drowning out my fear, I just needed to escape that house before they returned. I opened boxes and searched in drawers for anything, but came up empty. Returning to the window, I scanned the street, hoping to see someone. I flinched and stepped back from the window as their car pulled into the driveway.

Cursing under my breath, I realized the urgency of finding a weapon. With nothing in sight, I pried another slat from the headboard, the splintering wood releasing a musty scent. My intention wasn't murder, merely to incapacitate them temporarily so I could escape. I planned to hit Elias as soon as he walked in so I could sneak downstairs, find Mother, and catch her off guard with a sudden ambush. I needed time to unlock all those fucking bolts from the front door.

I heard Elias' footsteps approaching. Standing behind the door, I raised my arm, ready to strike. With the door opening, I held my breath, anticipating his arrival.

"We're back Cassie. Are you hungry? Mother is making us some sandwiches. Cassie, where are you?"

The minute I saw the back of his head, I swung with all my might. There was a loud thunk, and his body crumpled to the ground. I checked for a pulse. He was alive, but not moving. Stepping over him, I carefully began my descent down the creaking old wooden stairs. I crept along slowly, trying to keep my steps quiet so as not to alert Mother.

Since Elias said she was making us sandwiches, she must be in the kitchen. Arriving at the bottom, I looked at the front door. The urge to pick the locks was strong, but I knew I wouldn't finish before Mother heard the noise. I crept slowly down the main hallway to the kitchen. As she made sandwiches behind the island, she was positioned facing me. I pressed myself against the wall as she looked up; the slat held to my chest. I tried to slow my racing heart by taking several slow, deep breaths. The timing had to be perfect. It was now or never.

I peeked around the doorway again and didn't see her. Where did she go? I took a step forward, scanning the kitchen.

"Looking for me, dear?"

Spinning around at the unexpected sound of her voice, a shrill scream burst from my lips, a mix of fear and surprise. Just as I looked up, the bat swooped down towards my head.

# Chapter 24

# Devastation

## Sean

After I told Judy and Carl about Cassie, a wave of nausea washed over me as I blamed myself for Cassie's kidnapping. I promised them I would find Cassie come hell or high water and that was exactly what I was going to do. I drove to the police station and went straight into Chief Reyes office. Seated before the chief's desk was Detective Lucian Warrick.

"Did you find her?" I didn't even bother knocking.

"Have a seat." Chief Reyes pointed to the empty chair next to the detective.

Glancing at them both, I sat waiting for the update.

"Lucian and I have been searching for Elias. We don't have a last name yet, but we contacted our brothers at the sheriff's office on the mainland and they are helping us search. He doesn't show up as a local on our island, but we found several on the mainland. The sheriff's deputies are knocking on doors as we speak."

"Can I go with them?" My leg bounced, a frantic, uncontrollable motion betraying my anxiety. My girl was out there, and with every passing moment, I felt her life slipping away. The first 48 hours were critical; every minute felt heavy with consequence.

"You won't make it in time. They're already searching." Chief Reyes leaned his elbows on his desk and leaned forward. "I should receive a call soon, and we'll head out."

The waiting was killing me. "I can't just sit here. I gotta do something." I bolted out of the chair and paced the chief's office.

"You need to put on a uniform. Do you have one in your locker?" Lucian turned in his seat to face me.

"I do." I always kept a spare in my locker for emergencies like this one.

"Go put it on and meet me in the lounge. I'll start making some coffee for us." Lucian stood, pointing towards the door.

"I don't want coffee."

"Well, too fucking bad cause I do." Lucien pushed me out of the chief's office. "Get changed and meet me there."

"Does he want me out of there in case he gets bad news?" I said to Lucien over my shoulder.

"Maybe." Lucian shrugged.

We parted ways as I headed to my locker. I've never changed so fast before in my life. When I finished, I went to the lounge.

"Have a seat," Lucian said as he poured two black coffees into mugs. "You know, Chief is doing the best he can. He loves Cassie. He's known her since she was in diapers. Hell, we all love Cassie. The minute we hear anything from our brothers over the bridge, we're all getting in our cars and driving over there to hand that fucker his ass. "You can bet on that," he said, a glint in his eye. Setting both mugs down, Lucien sat across from him.

"Yeah, I get that," I grumbled. Of course, they all loved Cassie. She had told me how all the officers stopped by her café for a cup of coffee or two throughout the day. With both hands clasped around the steaming mug of coffee, I stared into the dark depths, the rich aroma filling my senses as I silently prayed for Elias to be found.

Lucian took a sip, then said. "Tell me what's spinning around in your head."

"It's my fault."

"Why do you think that?"

I wanted to make some friends in town. Over the past week, I realized just how much Lucian valued the chief and the other officers. With a shaky breath, I explained to him what happened with Kerri, Lynn, and Cassie.

"Shit man, that sucks." Lucian took another sip and leaned back in his chair.

"Yeah, I should've followed Cassie, but I didn't want to leave my sister alone with Kerri. And after Kerri left, I really thought Cassie would talk to me. And again." I threw my arms up in the air. "I didn't want to leave a thirteen-year-old alone. Fuck, what should I have done?"

"You were right not to leave your sister. It was a shitshow from the beginning. You need to know that Cassie has been burned by other guys before. Although she projects a strong, almost brazen demeanor, the truth is, she's incredibly sensitive and sweet. I'm sure this Elias creep knew that if he was watching her for as long as the chief suspects."

"I only saw him doing it this week, and I asked her to report him. But she said he was harmless, and I was blowing it out of proportion. She should've been with me and none of this would've happened."

"See." Lucian pointed at him. "That's where you're wrong."

"What are you talking about?" I squinted at him over my coffee cup.

"If this guy was so hell bent on getting her, he would've kept at it until he accomplished his goal. Psychopaths don't stop until they get what they want or who they want. I watched the video. I saw her looking around and being aware of her surroundings. Her body language tells me she wasn't totally trusting him. Didn't you notice how she kept a safe distance from him when they walked to his car? Her biggest mistake was reaching in for whatever was in there. If he hadn't drugged her, she would've fought back. I know Cassie. She wouldn't give up without a fight."

"I know you're right, but I'll feel a hell of a lot better when I can hold her in my arms and apologize." I mumbled.

"You got it bad, huh?" Lucian grinned.

"Yeah, she's the sweetest, smartest, sexiest girl I've ever dated and I want to spend the rest of my life putting a smile on her face and happiness in her heart."

"Wow. Great Hallmark card." Lucian smiled. "Remember those words when we get her back and you start groveling. She's gonna love that shit."

"I hope so, because if she doesn't love me back, I'll be devastated."

"Boys, let's roll!" Chief Reyes hollered from the hallway that led to the lounge.

Lucian and I jumped out of our chairs, leaving our coffee on the table.

# Chapter 25

# Til Death Do Us Part

## Elias

I woke up on the ground with a splitting headache. Sitting up, I reached back and felt a sticky, warm lump forming at the base of my skull. Was I bleeding? With a gasp, I pulled my hand forward; crimson blood, warm and slick, dripped from my fingertips. That's right. When I entered the room, Cassie was nowhere to be found on the bed. Judging from the splintered headboard, its broken pieces scattered on the floor, she must have been waiting for me, using one of the sharp slats as a weapon.

Furious, I stormed down the stairs. Mother would not be pleased to find out that Cassie got the jump on me. Rounding the corner on the first floor, I found Cassie slumped against the wall, legs spread wide, arms at her sides, blood streaming from a head wound. She looked like a Raggedy Ann doll someone had thrown against the wall. Mother was standing over her with the bat.

"Mother, what did you do?" I ran to Cassie and felt for a pulse. It was faint, but there.

"That little bitch tried to sneak up on me and hit me, but I showed her." Mother smiled wickedly. "I circled the dining room, crept up on her, and then hit her." Mother swung the bat, showing me how she did it.

"But we need her alive." I panicked.

"We can find another girl." Mother used the bat like a cane and leaned on it. "I don't like this one."

"But I like this one," I whined. Mother hated when I whined.

"Stop it." Mother released the bat and dropped to her knees in front of me. Cupping my jaw, she rained kisses all over my face. "Fine. I'll let you keep her. Is she alive?"

"Yes." I smiled at Mother.

Knock, knock, knock. "This is the Jones County Sheriff's Department. Please open the door."

We both froze and stared at each other.

"Take Cassie into our bedroom." Mother helped drape Cassie over my shoulder in a firefighter's carry. "Go into the closet and stay quiet. I'll take care of the police."

*** Mother ***

"Well, hello officer. What can I help you with?" I smiled as I answered the door.

"Ma'am, I'm from the Jones County Sheriff's Department. Does your son Elias live here?"

"No, sir. My son is old enough to live on his own."

"Do you have an address?"

"No, he moved recently and hasn't gotten around to sharing it with me. You know how boys are." I winked at the officer.

"Do you mind if I look around?"

"I am a woman who lives alone officer, I don't let anyone in. I'm sorry, but it pays to be careful." Asshole really thought I would let them enter my house.

"Sure, ma'am. I understand. If you talk to your son, can you tell him we're looking for him? He's not in any trouble. We just need to talk to him."

"Of course, but why are you looking for him?" I used my manners to be as nice as I could.

"There is a missing young lady from the island and we wanted to know if he'd seen her."

"Are you knocking on every door?" I had to get as much info as possible. "Why my son?"

"Someone thought Elias knew her from the island and might have spoken to her before she went missing."

"Oh well, they are mistaken. Elias doesn't go to Haven Island for coffee. He has great coffee shops here in town. I'm sure it's a case of mistaken identity."

"I'm sure you're right. Thank you for your time." The officer smiled and left her porch.

Closing the door, I checked my hair in the hall mirror. With that finally dealt with, I needed to check on the girl. I don't understand Elias's fascination with her, but if he truly wants her, I'll have to make her see things my way, even if I have to beat her into submission.

Chapter 26

# We Need a Plan

## Sean

"Chief!" I yelled as I ran toward him. "Did they find Cassie?"

"Yes. We need to kit up. Their SWAT team is joining ours, and we're meeting up in a couple of hours."

I followed Lucian and the chief to the weapons room. Several officers were already there, putting on their vests and checking their guns and ammunition. I hadn't done this here before. I didn't know where to go.

Hudson walked over. "Go over there and get a vest, gun, ammo and anything else you will need. Oh, and don't forget the helmet with night vision. We are breaching as soon as the warrant comes through, but it might be nightfall by then."

I followed Hudson's directions, ending up next to the chief.

"How do we know she's there?" I asked.

"Jones County Sheriff's Department received a call from a neighbor who said she saw someone in the house across the street screaming and banging on a second-floor attic window. The deputy closest to the call went to the caller's house and questioned her. She pointed to the house directly in front of hers and showed them which window. She apologized for not calling sooner, explaining that she had been scared. Just before approaching the house, the deputy realized it was on our list. He was cautious, yet certain the woman was lying; he even mentioned seeing blood in the hallway. The sheriff is waiting on a warrant to search the house and we are getting our asses in gear. Any more questions?"

"No, sir." I put an extra round of ammo in my vest.

"Then finish up. You're riding with me."

It seemed to take forever for everyone to get ready, but it was actually less than fifteen minutes. I ran into the chief's patrol vehicle, and we peeled out with lights and sirens blaring.

"Sean, I need you to keep your cool. If at any point you break protocol or a direct order, I will sideline you." Chief glanced my way. "Do you understand?"

"Yes, sir."

"I know how much you care about Cassie...," –I interrupted the chief. "I love her, sir."

"Yeah," Chief sighed. "That's what I thought from the way you look at her."

"What do you mean, the way I look at her?"

"All sappy and shit. Like a puppy dog waiting to be petted and loved."

"Damn," I sighed. "I didn't know I was that obvious."

"I was in the military and a police officer for most of my life. I see things others might miss. You...," Chief pointed at me. "Are pretty damn obvious with your love struck gaze when you're looking at her."

I guess I needed to work on my game face. Or not. If other officers noticed how much I loved her, they would keep their hands off of her. My face could work to my advantage.

"Wipe that smirk off your face," the Chief smiled. "We all know you love her and she's your girl. No one's gonna fuck with that."

"I take it you're a mind reader, too." I cocked my eyebrow at him.

Chief chuckled. "I wish. No, I'm not. But I have noticed the glare you give your fellow officers when they talk about flirting with Cassie at the café. They're just busting your balls. You know, new guy and all."

"Well, shit. Thanks for letting me know."

Pulling into the police parking lot one after another, they parked their cars side-by-side. The complex looked huge. It was one extensive building with several others to the side.

"If you ever have to come here." Chief pointed to the door directly in front of him. "You can swipe your badge at the door. Go straight past two offices, then go left and you will reach our comm center. All our calls go through them. There are offices, a couple of lounges, a workout room, and a large meeting room." Then the Chief pointed behind him. "Back there is our driving and shooting range. Technically, we are our own police force, but since the island is so small, we use them for comms and training."

I nodded, and we got out. Chief and I headed to where several officers and deputies stood by the Bearcat, the SWAT vehicle. It looked similar to the vehicle they call Black Betty on the television show SWAT. Except our Lenco Bearcat was a dark tan.

"Any updates?" Chief asked their officers.

"No, still waiting for a warrant, but we're kitted up and ready to roll." A deputy reached out to shake Chief's hand. "Good to see you, Chief."

"You too, Captain. Are you rolling with us?"

"You bet your ass I'm rolling out on this one." He smiled broadly at Chief Reyes.

"Happy to have you, Jay." Chief slapped his back. "It's been a while since we've been on a mission together."

"Rangers, lead the way, brother." Captain Jay slapped the chief's back.

I guess that answered my question about how the chief and the captain knew each other.

"Jay, this is Sean O'Reilly. He's new to our team as of Monday last week. He was a deputy down in South Florida."

"Nice to meet you, Sean." Captain Jay shook my hand and smiled. "Welcome to North Florida."

"Thank you, sir."

"Why did you go work for this asshole instead of me?" Captain Jay shoulder bumped the chief.

"I wanted a little more peace and quiet in my life." I answered wryly.

"How's that working out for you?" Captain Jay cocked his eyebrow.

"His girlfriend is the one that got kidnapped," Chief interjected.

Captain Jay's jaw dropped. "Shit, how are you holding up?"

"I'm keeping it tight. Or trying to anyway." Sean sighed.

"Let me go inside and see if they have news on that warrant." Captain Jay placed his hand on my shoulder. "I'll be back."

"I take it you both served together in the military?" I turned to Chief.

"Yep, 75th Ranger Regiment under U.S. Army Special Operations Command." Chief nodded. "You're in excellent hands. We will find Cassie and bring her home."

"Hey, Sean!" Lucian was waved at me. "Come here, meet the guys."

"Go ahead." Chief tilted his head toward Lucian. "I'm gonna follow Ray."

I jogged over to Lucian, and he introduced me to their SWAT officers, many of whom also did double duty in their department. As we were talking, a big ass SWAT officer walked our way. He looked mean as hell. When he approached, Lucian put his hand out, and they greeted each other.

"Sean, this mean ass mother fucker is Griffin although we all call him Cain, his under-cover name." Lucian smiled.

Cain smirked and gripped my hand in a firm handshake. Damn, I'm not a weak man. Shit, I got muscles and strength, but that man's hand engulfed mine like I was a little boy. He towered over me by at least five inches to my six-foot frame. Holy fuck, I would not want to see him mad.

"Nice to meet you, Cain." I firmed up my grip, and he chuckled.

All I could think about was when the Hulk called Loki a puny God. He was probably thinking puny officer.

"You, too."

"Coming with us, I see." Lucian pointed at his uniform, then turned to me. "Cain is usually in a pair of beat up jeans and t-shirt. He's rarely in uniform."

Cain held up a black nylon ski mask. "Gonna wear this, just in case."

"Alright. Listen up!" Chief was standing next to Captain Jay as the captain rounded up the troops. "We will have the warrant within the next thirty minutes, so let's roll out. The house is near a park. We'll hold there until we are a go. Make sure you have your night vision, cause that sun is dropping fast. I'll go over the dynamic entry once we get there."

Everyone jogged to their vehicles. I headed to the chief's and waited while he spoke to the captain. Then we drove to the park and gathered in front of the bearcat for our assignments.

Chapter 27

# Someone Please Help Me

## Cassie

I didn't know how long I'd been asleep. My head felt like someone was jack hammering into my skull. I couldn't move my arms and legs which were spread eagle. The bed felt different, softer, more comfortable. I opened my eyes, but shut them immediately because the pain that sliced through my head took my breath away. I relaxed my breaths and squinted, slowly opening my eyes again.

I was in an unfamiliar room. This one was bigger with nice antique furniture. As I scanned the room, I realized why I couldn't move my arms and legs. There was rope around my wrists and ankles, anchoring me to the bed's four posts. I tried to pull my arms and legs free, but there was no give. The rope was so tight, I could feel it cutting into my skin. Trying several more times, I stopped from the pain and the feel of blood trickling down around my wrists and ankles.

Glancing down, I saw I was wearing Mother's wedding dress. How had I not noticed when I looked at my feet? Panic set in. They had to have stripped me to put the dress on. What had they done to me? I closed my eyes and focused on the rest of my body, but could only feel pain and discomfort around my wrists, ankles, and head.

The last thing I remember was hiding just outside the doorway after I saw Mother in the kitchen. *Think Cassie, think,* I said to myself. Despite the agonizing headache, I pictured Mother at the plate, bat held, ready to strike like a seasoned batter. The bat whistled through the air before striking my head; the impact sending a wave of excruciating pain through me.

I shouldn't be alive. Wasn't that how they said Mother killed Elias' father? She must've only hit me hard enough to knock me out. But why? Why not just kill me? Not that I wanted to die. Then I remembered Elias saying his mother wanted grandchildren, but first we had to marry. Oh no, that's why I was wearing Mother's wedding dress. They were going to speed up the wedding so he could rape me and I could make her a grandmother.

"Help!" I screamed as loud as I could, pulling on the ropes, praying for a miracle. Tears streaming down the sides of my face, I continued to pull and scream until the door swung open.

"Shut up, you ungrateful woman." Mother stormed into the room and slapped me hard across the face. "Stop fighting the rope. You are getting blood on my beautiful gown and all over my sheets."

I didn't stop. Fuck her gown and sheets. Clearly, she cared about both because she punched me in the stomach. A searing pain doubled me over, each breath a fresh wave of agony as I gasped for air. The rope bit deeper into my skin, each tightening pull a burning brand.

"Why are you doing this to me?" I moaned.

"Don't be stupid. I've already told you I want grandchildren and my son chose you." Mother huffed.

"But, why me?" Turning my head, her hateful stare confronted me; her eyes seemed to pierce me with icy malice.

"Because my son chose you. He thinks you are beautiful and I need him to be attracted to you so you can mate."

"But I don't want to mate with your son." I murmured.

"Blasphemy!" Mother slapped me again. "Stop talking like that or I will cut your tongue out."

"Mother, what's going on?" Elias stepped into the room. "I only stepped out to light the candles for our ceremony." Elias walked up to the bed.

"She's an ungrateful woman, Elias." Mother approached him and French kissed him right in front of me. I wanted to gag as I watched them roam their hands all over each other. Please, dear God, let them take their psychotic love somewhere else.

"Elias, look at what she'd done to my dress." Mother pointed to my feet.

Elias picked up the bottom of the dress and threw the hem up away from my ankles. "There. Now it can't get any more blood on it." Then he ran his hands over Mother's face before cupping it and kissing her. "Better now?"

"Yes, my love. She's ready for you. I bathed and shaved her before I dressed her."

What the hell? Did she just say what I think she said? She shaved me. Did she shave my nether region? I pulled at the ropes again.

"I told you to stop that!" Mother screamed, but Elias grabbed her hand before she struck me again.

"Mother, we need her awake for the ceremony. Why don't we go downstairs and set everything up? It's getting dark."

After more kissing and feeling each other up, they left the room. My stomach was cramping violently; a bitter taste of bile burned the back of my throat. As soon as I turned my head, I vomited. Shit, Mother would not like that, I thought before a fit of laughter turned into hysteria.

Chapter 28

# I'm Coming Cassie...Hold On

## Sean

"We have the warrant. When we get to the house. I want no lights and sirens. Several of you are setting perimeters around the entire block while SWAT goes in. Make sure your radio is on and let's keep each other updated as we go. Cain, go in and do some recon. SWAT, wait one house north of the suspect's house until I give the signal. Let's go." Captain Jay raised his arm over his head and spun it around. "Wheels up, boys!"

Again, I followed Chief Reyes.

"Sean, let SWAT do their thing. As soon as Cassie is secured, you can go in." Chief said as he drove us to the end of the block.

"Sir, please." I turned and pleaded. "I've been on missions with SWAT. Let me breach with them."

Chief sighed, "I don't think it's a good idea."

"If it was your woman in there." I pointed down the street. "Wouldn't you want to be there?"

"Yeah." Chief nodded and turned to me. Pointing in my face, he said, "But watch your six and listen to the SWAT commanding officer."

"Copy that, sir." I nodded, and we both exited the vehicle.

I ran toward the SWAT leader with the chief. "Bobby." Chief pointed at me. "He's with you. He knows you're in charge."

"Got it, sir." Bobby nodded and shook my hand. "Glad to have you."

I jogged out with Bobby and the team. When we reached our location, we crouched down waiting for the signal.

Over the headset, I heard everyone checking in with their positions. Then came Cain's deep, low voice.

"House is empty. An older lady, Elias, and Cassie, are in the backyard. Cassie's hands are bound behind her back. Someone shackled her legs with a rope to prevent her from running. The older lady is standing in front of them. Looks like a fucking wedding ceremony with the older lady presiding. Elias is holding a rope with a noose around Cassie's neck. We gotta be careful, boys. If he pulls hard enough, he could snap her neck. Someone call the fire department because when the shit hits the fan, if anyone knocks over any of the zillion fucking candles burning on the ground, it's gonna go up fast. I'm gonna sneak around and position myself close to Elias. Come in quietly."

My mind was spinning. Cassie must be so scared. I noticed Cain didn't say anything about how she looked. Had they hurt her? She must not be drugged if she was standing on her own. But fuck, having a noose around your neck sure would make your life flash before you. And why the fuck was there a wedding ceremony? There were so many pieces missing from this story. Yet the only piece he wanted was Cassie, safe in his arms.

"Okay," Cain mumbled. "I'm in place. We go on three. One."

We all moved stealthily as a team to the front of Elias' house. Bobby motioned with his hands for the two groups to surround the house on both sides. I followed behind Bobby.

"Two."

Bobby slowly unlocked the gate to the backyard fence, and we paused.

"Three, go, go, go." I could hear Cain running and shouting police freeze.

We all ran in at the same time. I saw Cain come up behind Elias and wrap one hand around his throat while the other squeezed his hand until he released the rope. As I ran to Cassie, the older woman threw her Bible at an approaching officer and dove for the rope. Her momentum pulled Cassie down and tightened the rope around her neck, knocking over several candles around them.

"No, no! Cassie!" I screamed. The fire was so close to her hair and the fucking rope was choking her. Her eyes bugged out as she gasped in horror while the flames grew around them.

"Ma'am, let go of the rope." Bobby screamed.

"No, if she is not marrying my son, then she will die!" the woman pulled on the rope.

Bobby pointed the gun at her forehead. "I said, let go of the fucking rope!"

"Cassie!" I yelled again. But I wasn't sure she could hear me. Her face was turning red. I wanted to run to her, but Lucian held me back.

"Mother! Let go of the rope and get away from the fire!" Elias screamed while Cain held his arm and cuffed him.

"Don't touch my son!" Mother yelled at Cain and released her grip on the rope.

That was all the distraction the officers closest to Cassie needed. An officer grabbed the rope and pulled it out of Mother's hands. Lucian released me and I ran to Cassie. Dropping to the ground, I loosened the knot around her throat. She coughed and took several gasps of air. Taking the noose off her head. I pulled her body away from the fire and onto my lap. I could hear the fire engines coming to put out the fire.

"I love you, Cassie." I kissed her forehead and pulled her to my chest. "Shit, I thought I'd lost you."

"Sean, I..," Cassie's voice croaked.

"Shh, don't talk, just catch your breath." Someone tapped my shoulder. Chief handed me an open bottle of water for Cassie. I took the bottle and pressed it against Cassie's lips. "Cass, it's water. Take a couple sips." I tipped the bottle to her lips while Chief untied her hands. Captain Jay was working on the rope wrapped around her ankles. The firefighters ran over with the hose and put out the fire. Thank fuck, Cain had said, to call the fire department.

As soon as her hands were free, she wrapped them around my neck and cried as I held her tightly against me. I rubbed her back and kept murmuring, "It's okay. You're okay. I'm here. I'll take you home."

When I kissed her forehead and ran my fingers through her hair. I felt a lump on the back of her head.

"Chief." I looked up at him. "She needs medical attention. She has an enormous lump on the back of her head."

"On it." Chief stood and yelled, "I need medical help!"

I saw two paramedics hauling ass toward us with a gurney. I picked her up and laid her on the gurney. Then Cassie's hand shot out, fingers brushing against mine before she pulled me down toward her, her touch surprisingly strong.

"Cass, it's gonna be okay."

"Don't leave me," she whispered before she coughed.

"Okay, baby." I wiped the tears from her face and looked directly into her eyes. "I'll go with you."

"This man is riding with you." Chief said to the paramedics. "Where are you going?"

"Jones Health Hospital."

"I'll meet you there, Sean. Take care of our girl," Chief said as they wheeled Cassie to the ambulance while I held her hand.

"You bitch! Look what you did!" Elias' mother continued to scream at Cassie.

"Get her out of here! Now!" Chief hollered to the officers who cuffed the older lady.

# Chapter 29

# Everything Hurts

## Cassie

I woke up in another unfamiliar bed, the rhythmic beeping of machines and the hushed murmuring of voices I recognized nearby filling the air. My entire body was sore, but I wasn't in as much pain as before. Opening my eyes, I looked down at the IV in my arm and smiled. I was on good meds, hence the slight discomfort, but no pain.

"Cassie, my baby!" My mom ran to me, tears streaming down her face, her sobs audible even above the surrounding noise. "We were so worried about you."

"I'm okay now, mom, thanks to Sean and the officers." I smiled at Sean.

"Oh, honey, we're so glad you're okay." Dad grabbed my other hand and kissed it.

"If you're here...," I squinted at them, "who's running the restaurant?"

"We closed it. We put a sign on the door that said 'Sorry, family emergency'." Mom kissed my forehead. "Seeing you is more important that the restaurant."

"Thanks, mom."

Mom wiped her face with a tissue and looked behind her at Sean. "We'll give you two a few minutes." Mom waved at dad to follow her.

Sean moved close to the bed and ran his finger over the back of my hand.

"Cass. I'm so sorry. This was all my fault." Sean's voice was low and sorrowful.

"Hey." I intertwined our fingers and gently pulled him until he sat on the edge of the bed. "I'm okay, thanks to you and my friends in blue." I smiled.

Sean ran his finger from his other hand lightly over the bandages on my wrist and neck. "You never would've been in that situation if you hadn't seen what you did."

"That night…," I was going to continue, but Sean placed his finger on my lips.

"Let me get this out." He pushed some strands of hair off my face. "Kerri tricked my sister Lynn into bringing her to me. I never told Lynn that Kerri had cheated on me or how I found out because Lynn liked Kerri. I didn't care if they remained friends, but I didn't want to ever see Kerri again. Anyway, when you arrived Kerri was trying to get back together, and I'd told her no way in hell. But then she kissed me. I swear, Cass, I never kissed her back. I didn't even open my mouth. Her actions disgusted me."

Sean raised our intertwined hands and kissed the back of my hand.

"I made it clear she needed to leave, and she did. Unfortunately, it stranded my sister at my house. I would've gone looking for you sooner, but Lynn is only thirteen and I didn't want to leave her alone in a strange house. I tried to call and text you. I wanted to apologize. I'm ready to do all the groveling you want me to do."

I smiled at Sean. "I don't need you to grovel. Although, I do like the idea of you on your knees."

"I would like that too," Sean smiled wickedly.

"I went to the park to think. I was on my way back to you to hear your side and fight for you when Elias injected me with something and took me." I closed my eyes. "I've never been so scared before in my life."

"Hey." Sean softly kissed my lips. "They're both in jail. They can't get to you."

I nodded and opened my eyes.

"You were going to fight Kerri for me?" Sean smirked.

"Jerk." I shoved his chest. "I was hoping it wouldn't come to that, but yeah, I'd throw a punch for you." I smiled.

"There's that smile I love. You never have to throw a punch for me because I would never do anything that would warrant that." Sean leaned in and cupped my face. "I love you, Cass."

"I love you, too. Now kiss me like you mean it."

"Yes, ma'am."

# Chapter 30

# Epilogue

## Sean

Once Cassie got out of the hospital, she went back to her parent's house. I wanted her to come and stay with me, but I had to work during the day and her mom and sister took shifts helping her. So I visited every day after work and stayed until dark.

Even as adults, the idea of sleeping with Cassie in her bedroom felt like a betrayal, a profound disrespect to her parents. Cassie and I decided to move in together once she'd recovered. As she felt better, I moved her stuff into my house and we shopped for a King size bed for the master bedroom. I hadn't proposed, but I already had her father's approval and the ring was in my pocket. My best friend George had come up and returned the favor of going ring shopping. Lizzy and Cassie got along great and we couldn't wait until George and Lizzy came back for a longer stay. We promised them we'd get rid of the twin beds and put at least a queen-size one in the spare room. Not that they complained. Lizzy just pushed the beds together.

Tonight was our first night in our home, and I was making dinner. Katie was dropping Cassie off in a few minutes. I had everything ready. The table was set, and the food was ready. Instead of grilling, I made a lasagna that was cooling on top of the stove. I considered putting candles on the table, but worried they'd be a painful reminder of that awful night. Instead, I placed a small vase of flowers in the center.

"Honey, we're home!" Katie hollered from the hallway.

I had already given Cassie her key to the house. Stepping out of the kitchen, I saw Cassie shove Katie and laugh.

"Hey Katie." I wiped my hands on a kitchen towel and draped it over my shoulder. "Thanks for bringing Cassie." I reached for Cassie. "Hi baby, welcome home." Then I kissed the living daylights out of her.

"That's my cue to go. Have fun!" Katie swung the door shut.

Cassie ran her fingers through my hair before she pulled her mouth away. "It's smells good in here."

"Mm." I leaned down and ran my tongue from her jaw to her neck. "You smell better."

"Have you missed me?" Cassie pressed against me, her hands caressing my shoulders and back.

"Fuck, yeah." I embraced her tightly while kissing her deeply. "I missed worshipping your body and making love to you."

"I've missed you, too." One of Cassie's hands slid between us to cup my groin.

I had to put a stop to this speeding train if I wanted to have a nice dinner.

"Oh, baby." Pulling my lips away from hers, I reached for her hands and pulled them away from me. "I'm gonna feed you before we play."

Cassie intertwined our fingers and pushed her hips against mine while her mouth sought another kiss. "Am I gonna need my energy for later?"

I released one of her hands and slapped her ass. "You better believe your ass you will."

We laughed as we pulled apart.

"Mm, spanking." Cassie jumped up on the counter and spread her legs. "I might like that."

Groaning, I carefully used potholders to grab the lasagna. "Come on, my little sex vixen. Let's go eat."

Cassie jumped down from the counter and followed me to the dining table. "Wow, that looks nice."

I set down the lasagna and pulled out a chair for her. "Your seat."

"Why, thank you." Cassie placed a kiss on my cheek and sat.

I poured the wine, and we ate our meal, talking about other things we needed for the house. When we finished the lasagna, I pulled out ice cream for dessert. Except her ice cream had a special sparkle to it.

I placed the two scoops of cookies and cream with whipped cream in front of her. The engagement ring sat at the top instead of a cherry.

"Oh, my God! Sean!" Cassie's eyes widened, and she covered her mouth with both hands.

As I got down on one knee before her, I reached over and pulled her hands away from her face so I could hold them.

"Cass, I love you. No if, ands, buts, or maybes. I'm head over heals in love with you. I moved to this island looking for a future and I found it the minute I entered that restaurant and set my eyes on you. You are a beautiful, intelligent, caring woman. I'd never thought I would find everything I wanted in one girl, but you proved me wrong. You are my forever, and I can't wait to turn this house into a home with you and our future children. Will you marry me?"

"Yes! Yes!" Cassie bounced in her seat.

I stood and pulled her into my arms. Devouring her mouth like my life depended on her. "I love you," I murmured against her lips.

"I love you, too." Cassie said between kisses. "You know, that ring is probably really sticky from the whipped cream."

"Oh, I have an idea about that. Wrap your legs around me. It's dessert time."

I grabbed the bowl of ice cream and carried my love into our bedroom. We made quick work of our clothes and I showed her what a great spoon the ring was as I covered her body with whipped cream and ice cream, making her my ice cream sundae dessert.

Book 2 in this series is Chief Alejandro.
To read Alejandro and Sammie's story, click here:
https://a.co/d/9EFoQ66

# Chapter 31

# Thank You!

This prequel smoothly transitions readers from my "Path Series" to the exciting new adventures in "Haven Island PD, Protecting Paradise," creating a satisfying link between the two. Although each book in the series is a standalone novel, expect to see familiar faces from Haven Island populating the pages of each one. Keep an eye out for the surprise cameos of beloved Path Series characters throughout the books.

Thank you to all my readers–You are the BEST! I am beyond grateful for all of your continued support.

A special thank you to Michelle K and Michelle Z. They read all my pre-published books and help me make them better.

I could not have written this book without the help of several people. If I got anything wrong or applied creative license, it is my doing. Their insightful feedback and extensive knowledge helped shape my story into something better.

I feel blessed and honored to know the following first responders. As I write my chapters and questions arise, I reach out to them via text, email, or phone call and they ALWAYS respond with answers as quickly as they can. The Best Men in Blue Support Team ever: Sargeant TJ Williams, K9 Deputy Bryan Wright, and Corrections Deputy Nathan Lebon.

To all the first responders out there, the ones I'm blessed to call my friends and those I haven't met, please stay safe out there. It can be a little crazy. Thank you, thank you, thank you, for what you do for all of us in your community daily.

I know my books are hard to find because I lack reviews, but if you follow me on Amazon as one of your favorite authors, you'll receive alerts when I release a book.

# Chapter 32

# About the Author

Neri Lopez has worn many hats as a stay-at-home mom of triplets, graphic designer, and high school teacher (Spanish, Art, and Graphic Design). She lives in Florida with her husband, grown kids, and their fur babies, Mocha and Chewy. She is a crafter of all trades, including crocheting (several craft shows a year), jewelry making, scrapbooking, knitting, sewing, and painting.

Neri loves to hear from her readers, contact her at: sirenbookandcraft@gmail.com

**For a simple way to access her books through QR codes, go to her website: sirenbookandcraft.com**

(When you sign up for her newsletter, you will receive a FREE downloadable bookmark of Red Path.)

Please consider writing a review on Amazon and/or Goodreads after you read Neri's books. It helps her books be more visible on Amazon.

Or follow her on:

**facebook: Neri Lopez - Author**

**instagram: Neri_Lopez_Author**

*(She is most active on facebook)*

**The Path Series (available on Amazon)**

**Book 1: Red Path** (Thunder and Isa)

**Book 2: Unconquered Path** (Alex and Tori)

**Book 3: Wagering Path** (Holt and Freya)

**Book 4: Unexpected Path** (Mark and Maggie)

**Novella Book 4.5: Double Trouble Path**

(Maggie and Freya's weddings)

**Book 5: Twisted Path** (Barrett and Angel)

**Book 6: Blue Path** (George and Lizzy)

www.ingramcontent.com/pod-product-compliance
Lightning Source LLC
Chambersburg PA
CBHW030942310726
48969CB00008B/2344